A DARK SHADOW FALLS

A DCI DANI BEVAN NOVEL

BY

KATHERINE PATHAK

THE GARANSAY PRESS

Books by Katherine Pathak

The Imogen and Hugh Croft Mysteries:

Aoife's Chariot

The Only Survivor

Lawful Death

The Woman Who Vanished

Memorial for the Dead
(Introducing DCI Dani Bevan)

The Ghost of Marchmont Hall

Short Stories:

Full Beam

DCI Dani Bevan novels:

Against A Dark Sky

On A Dark Sea

A Dark Shadow Falls

The Garansay Press

The Garansay Press

PROLOGUE

An unassuming black Ford Focus pulled onto the driveway of a modern semi-detached property in the heart of a non-descript estate. Lyle Murphy sighed heavily before shifting his weight around and climbing out of the driver's seat.

The evening was windy and cold. Lyle glanced up at the house and noted it was in darkness. He wondered where Morna could possibly be. Wherever she was, her absence meant there'd be no dinner waiting for him. After the awful day he'd just had, this felt like the final insult.

He turned his key in the lock and what immediately struck the man, as he stepped inside, was that it was just as cold in the hallway as it was out front. Lyle shrugged off his jacket and dumped his briefcase in the porch. As he went into the kitchen, he identified the source of the fierce draft whistling through the house. The back door was wide open, its top pane of glass broken into numerous pieces now scattered across the garden patio.

'Morna!' He called out warily, almost tip-toeing into the living room at the rear.

There were no lights on anywhere in the place. This room was a mess. The television set was gone. The sofa had been upturned and magazines and papers lay strewn across the carpet. Lyle looked feverishly about him, turning on his heels and jogging up the stairs. 'Are you here, darling? What's happened?'

Lyle kicked open the door to their bedroom. He stood perfectly still on the threshold, gripping the frame with both hands.

His wife was lying face down on the double-bed, her blondish hair splayed out all around her. Lyle took a few tentative steps towards Morna, the carpet squelching under his feet. With a monumental effort of willpower, he edged closer. He identified a number of puncture wounds across his wife's back. The carpet and bed-clothes were saturated with her blood.

Lyle rested his hand on her bare arm, which was hanging limply by her side. The skin was stone cold. He fell to his knees on the damp floor, totally aware that he was contaminating himself and the scene. The man closed his eyes tight shut, half-hoping that whoever had done this to Morna was still in the house and was merciful enough to come back into the room and finish the job.

Chapter 1

The wind had finally died down. Huw Bevan's substantial bungalow was west facing and took the brunt of the weather blowing in off the Atlantic Ocean. Dani's father had recently fitted his windows with triple-glazing that kept out the worst of the chill. His wood-burner heated the open-plan living spaces extremely efficiently.

Dani's only objection to the wind was that when the gusts were at their fiercest, it became impossible to venture along the huge expanse of flat, yellow sand in the cove just a stone's throw from her father's house. Dani Bevan had been on Colonsay for a week already and had only managed to take their border terrier out a couple of times for a run on the beach. The poor thing was going stir crazy.

'I'm taking Gillespie out for a walk,' she called into her father's study. The man grunted something inaudible in reply.

Dani pulled on her thick jacket and woolly hat. She made sure the dog was securely on his lead before closing the front door and heading down to the shore. The sun was beginning to set over the clear blue water. As soon as Dani was through the gate, onto the sand, she let Gillespie run free and breathed in the crisp air as he shot off into the water.

Bevan must have strolled into an area with better mobile reception as the phone in her pocket began buzzing insistently. Dani glanced at the screen, noting she had half a dozen messages on her voice mail. She rested her weight on a rock and held the phone to her ear, patiently listening to each one. In her line of work, staying in a place where she was almost impossible to reach suited Bevan very well. She wouldn't be able to get a proper break otherwise. Her last case had really taken it out of her and had given Dani reason to question her own judgement. The DCI wouldn't be returning to Pitt Street until she knew she was completely ready.

One of the messages had piqued her interest. The rest were requests for paperwork from members of Bevan's department. She would e-mail the relevant officers later. For the time being, Dani concentrated on watching Gill chasing his own tail in the crashing surf and savouring the golden sunset which provided the stunning backdrop to this ludicrous performance.

Huw Bevan was making a start on dinner when Dani returned to the house. She gave Gill a rub down with the towel they kept by the back door. The dog made a bee-line for his basket.

'Did you see anyone whilst you were out?' Huw asked, heaping a handful of green beans into the steamer.

'I saw Jilly O'Keefe at her kitchen window. She was watching the birds settling on the headland. I gave her a wave.' Dani dropped into one of the seats.

'She would have been cursing Gill for scaring off the wildlife, I expect.'

Dani smiled. 'It's quiet enough most of the time. I'm sure she wouldn't begrudge a poor wee dog some exercise.'

'Not normally, but we've had more visitors to our little bay than usual of late.' Huw turned up the light under the vegetables and took the chair opposite his daughter. The man possessed a mop of silver hair and a lean physique. He was aged in his late sixties but still fit and active. 'The landowner has sold off the old bothy beside Jilly's place. They've had 4x4s and contractors up there on a regular basis for the past month. It'll get a total refit and then be used for weekends.'

'Let's hope the disruption's only temporary.' Dani fiddled with the phone in her hand, finally placing it down on the oak table between them. 'Have you heard of Eric Fisher?'

Huw narrowed his eyes, thinking carefully about this. 'I'm not sure,' he replied.

'He was the man who killed his wife and children at their home in Dalkeith last year. Fisher's trial starts in a couple of weeks.'

'Oh yes, I remember the case. It was an awful tragedy.'

Dani nodded. 'I've had a message from an associate of mine, someone I've worked with in the past. Her name is Sally Irving-Bryant QC. She's representing Fisher at the trial.'

'What does she want with you? The case occurred well outside your jurisdiction.'

'Sally would like us to meet up. She wants my advice, which means the defence team must be really struggling.' Dani sighed heavily. 'I'm not surprised.'

'In those sorts of circumstances, the defence usually claim a temporary loss of sanity. I suspect there's a mental health issue. The man must have totally taken leave of his senses to do something like that.'

Dani ran a hand through her neat crop of dark hair, thinking through the details of the case, which had been reported widely across Scotland.

It was what American psychologists referred to as 'family annihilation' but Dani's department in Glasgow preferred to term, 'domestic homicide'. The family were discovered by a neighbour, who'd heard the commotion through their shared wall.

Peggy Fisher was found lying in the hallway. She'd been stabbed several times in the chest with a knife from the kitchen. Callum, who was twelve years old, was discovered in his bedroom. There'd clearly been a tussle in there between father and son. Callum had received defensive wounds to his hands and arms but was killed by a knife wound to the back which pierced his heart.

The three year old twins, Kyla and Skye, had been drowned in the bath. The knife hadn't been used in the bathroom at all. No blood traces were evident in this room.

Eric Fisher was found in the kitchen, slumped against a cupboard. The knife was still in his hand. The man had taken a handful of pills and attempted to cut his own throat, passing out before the job was complete. There was plenty of blood though. The thin linoleum was stained crimson and the neighbour slipped over in it whilst trying to reach Eric to check if he was still alive.

Fisher was taken to hospital. After a few rough days, when his health was touch and go, he slowly began to recover. Eric Fisher wasn't able to go on remand for six months. Now, the man was finally considered fit to stand trial.

The case had been handled by the eastern division. Dani knew they'd pulled out all the stops. An expert was flown in from the States, where the police had more experience of these types of domestic crime. Bevan really wasn't sure what Sally thought she could contribute. Dani had no expertise in the area at all.

Huw looked at his daughter closely. 'Try not to think about it whilst you're here. This visit is supposed to be stress free.'

'Of course,' Dani said, getting up and reaching for a bottle of wine. 'Is this one okay to have with dinner?' She enquired of her father, rummaging in a drawer for the opener.

Chapter 2

Sally Irving-Bryant was an attractive blond in her late forties. She'd been a lawyer for over twenty years, like her father was before her. Sally's younger brother was a solicitor. But she and her dad forged their careers at the criminal bar, both of them earning a formidable reputation as tenacious advocates.

Sally's desk was always well organised. Her case notes were stored in separate colour coded files and she prided herself on never mislaying a piece of evidence. On this particular morning, the lawyer had laid out all the papers relating to the Fisher case on the desk in front of her.

The crime scene photographs were disturbing, the very worst being those of the Fishers' two little girls, Kyla and Skye. Despite the rest of the images containing copious amounts of blood, the sight of the girls' poor lifeless bodies, half submerged in the water, in an environment which should have been safe and nurturing, had haunted Sally's dreams for months. For the first time in her long career, this case was seriously testing her resolve.

Her mobile phone began to ring. It was her husband, Grant Bryant, the CEO of Bryant Construction, one of the largest building firms in Scotland. She immediately took the call.

'We've had a sudden break in the weather, darling,' he announced. 'If you still want to make that trip, now's the time.'

'Great, I certainly do. I'll be with you in forty-five minutes,' Sally's voice displayed her ill-disguised relief.

*

It was early April, but taking a small aircraft out to the Western Isles was still a risky venture. Grant Bryant had a private helicopter based at an airfield in Helensburgh. His firm specialised in eco-builds in some of the most inaccessible parts of Scotland. He often had to fly to these remote places in order to view the progress on a site. When his wife pulled up at the helipad in her BMW, Grant strode across the tarmac to greet her.

He kissed her on the lips. 'The chopper's ready. Do you want me to come with you?'

She shook her head. 'No, it's fine. I'll only need an hour or so, then I'll be heading back.'

Grant gazed up at the sky. 'You may only have that. The tower has told us we've got a window of five hours max before the weather closes in again.'

'I'd better get going, then.' She reached for her briefcase and walked towards the helicopter, allowing her husband to help her into the passenger seat.

Grant stood well back, his hands on his hips, watching the machine take to the air and hover briefly above him before it proceeded due west, on a direct course towards the Isle of Colonsay.

*

Making the most of the good conditions, Dani and her father had walked around Kiloran Bay and were aiming to drive to the Colonsay Hotel in Scalasaig for lunch. But as they approached the house, Dani made out a figure up ahead, standing by the stone wall. As they got closer, the detective recognised the woman's even features and discerned her formal attire. She looked as if she'd stepped straight out of an Edinburgh courtroom. The sight was quite disconcerting amongst the bleak beauty of this picturesque and remote spot.

'I'm so sorry to interrupt your holiday,' Sally announced, as soon as the walkers were within earshot. 'I arrived by helicopter about ten minutes ago. I knew you couldn't be far away.'

'We saw the chopper,' Dani declared. 'We thought a boat might be in trouble on the water.'

'Oh no, nothing like that.' The lawyer flashed them a reassuring smile.

'Please come inside,' Huw offered, opening the door for their guest. 'I assume you'll be staying for lunch?'

'Just a quick bite, thank you, Mr Bevan. I'll need to get back to the mainland soon.'

Dani led the woman into the large living room, inviting her to take a seat by the picture window, which enjoyed uninterrupted views out to sea.

'My goodness. It feels as if we're on the edge of the world,' Sally commented quietly.

'Although people are still perfectly capable of following me here, it would seem,' Dani replied dryly.

She grimaced. 'I'm sorry about that.' Sally leant forward, knitting her fingers together and revealing a set of glossy, dark-red nails. 'I'll be honest with you, Dani. I'm in trouble with this case I'm defending.'

Huw came into the room with two mugs of tea, setting them down carefully on the coffee table and returning to the kitchen.

'What is Eric Fisher like?' Dani asked with genuine interest.

'He's a very complicated character. I find him *impossible* to read. That's my problem.'

'What is his plea?'

'Not guilty.'

Dani took a sip of tea, raising her eyebrows in surprise.

'He claims that someone *else* was in the house

with them that Sunday afternoon.'

'Was there any sign of a break-in?'

'There was nothing mentioned in the police report. No locks had been forced and no prints were found other than the family's. But then Fisher didn't make his claim about an intruder until he'd properly regained consciousness, which was several weeks later. It wasn't a line of inquiry that the police were focussing on in the hours and days after the murders.'

'So what is Fisher's account of the events?' Dani shifted forward in her seat, her interest definitely piqued.

'Eric and Callum arrived back from football training at 3pm. The girls were playing out in the garden whilst Peggy Fisher unpegged the washing from the line. The boys sat down and watched television in the front room. Half an hour later, Peggy brought Kyla and Skye back in, complaining that they were muddy. She ran the girls a bath. Eric was given the job of supervising them in the water.

Peggy went into the kitchen to start preparing dinner for the children. Eric went up to the bathroom. After he'd put the girls into the bubble bath, Eric heard a scream from downstairs. He didn't want to leave the children unattended so he shouted to his wife, asking what was wrong. He heard no more from her.

Eric got the girls washed as quickly as he could, shampooing and rinsing their hair. He intended to lift them out and then see what had happened to his wife. He thought maybe she'd burnt her hand on the iron, or something.

Before he got the chance, Eric was grappled from behind and dragged out of the bathroom. Someone shoved him into the airing cupboard, squashing him up next to the tank and then barring the door shut.

Fisher was shouting and hammering but couldn't get out.'

'Did he get a look at this *so-called* intruder?'

Sally sighed. 'No. The attacker was dressed in black, with a dark hoodie pulled low over his face. Eric claims he heard his son and this man fighting. It lasted no longer than a few minutes. After this, there was a short silence before the cupboard door was opened. A hood of some kind was placed over Eric's head and he was dragged down the stairs. The man put a knife to his throat and forced him to swallow pills, one by one. Then he felt the blade slice across his neck. That's the last thing he recalls. The problem for me is that he's sticking to this story religiously. If I could put in a plea of reduced responsibility, we might have a chance of mitigation. As it stands, Eric Fisher is looking at four life sentences. He's shown no sign of remorse so if he's found guilty he hasn't got a hope in hell of parole.'

'Is he upset about what happened to his wife and children?'

'Yes, of course, but he's angry more than anything else. Eric claims he wants to find out who did this to his family. Our psychiatrist thinks Fisher is just in total denial. If the expert witness can't even help us, we're in serious trouble.'

Chapter 3

They ate lunch at the kitchen table. Sally kept glancing nervously out of the window at the clouds blowing in off the darkening water.

'Was anything taken from the house?' Dani asked, sipping from a spoonful of watercress soup.

'Nothing obvious. But Eric hasn't been allowed back to the place since he was arrested, so he's not had a chance to look around properly.'

'His word wouldn't really have any credence though, not if all the principal items of value were untouched. It couldn't help his case even if he did spot something missing.'

Sally threw her arms up in the air. 'I haven't got a great deal of time, Dani. I realise the murders didn't occur within your jurisdiction but I'd like you to check if the intruder scenario was ever properly investigated.' The woman began counting off points on her fingers. 'Was the cupboard on the landing swabbed for Eric's prints? Were there any traces of the hood Eric claimed to have over his head in the neck wound or on his clothing? Did the neighbours see anyone suspicious entering or leaving the property that day?'

'Why would I do that, Sally?'

The woman rested her hands palm up on the table. 'I've represented plenty of guys who I knew were guilty as sin. I've never had a problem with it before. This case is different. I have no idea if Eric Fisher killed his family or not and I've spent countless hours with the man. But there's something about this crime which has profoundly unsettled me - as if a force of evil was at work in that house. I can't explain it, Dani. I just need your help.'

The detective turned towards her father, who shrugged his shoulders in a non-committal gesture. 'Okay,' she announced, pushing back her chair. 'Give me ten minutes to pack a bag. Is there room in that chopper for another passenger?'

*

Bevan had promised Sally Irving-Bryant that she would spend a couple of days in Glasgow, checking out the Fisher case before meeting the lawyer in Edinburgh for an update. Dani deposited her bags at her flat in Scotstounhill and proceeded straight to the Pitt Street offices.

As she strode across the floor of the serious crime division in her walking trousers and fleece, several of her officers glanced up in surprise.

'Good afternoon,' she announced brusquely, hoping to get twenty minutes of breathing space before the hordes descended.

This hope was swiftly dashed. DS Phil Boag followed her into the office and pulled the door shut behind him.

'Hello, Ma'am. It's great to see you. We weren't expecting you back until next week.'

'Well, I'm not here officially. I just wanted to grab some paperwork to take home.'

Phil didn't pick up on the hint. 'DCS Nicholson has sent Andy to Irvine on a week long course - something about working harmoniously in a team.'

Dani burst out laughing. 'I bet he's loving that!'

'He's been calling me every day, each time sounding increasingly desperate. Andy is convinced that Nicholson waited until you were on leave to set this up. He wants me to manufacture a crisis back here so that he can be sent home.'

Bevan was still chuckling. 'Well, I owe the guy a favour. He did save my life a few months ago.'

Phil smiled, 'sadly, there's no hint of a crisis. We're currently working on last Saturday's break-in at the lock-ups on the Rutherglen Industrial Estate. It's hardly life or death. Alice Mann and I have got it well covered.'

Dani became serious again. 'What do you know about the Fisher murders, over in Dalkeith?'

'Only what I read in the papers. I've got a DI friend at City and Borders. I know he was involved in the original investigation.'

'Would you mind if I got in touch with him? I need a contact over there. I'm going to be spending the next few days reviewing the case materials. I could actually really do with Andy Calder's help to sift through them.'

'I'll give you Mike's number, if you like?'

'Great, and leave the Andy problem with me, Phil. I'll speak to Nicholson and get something sorted.'

'Thanks, Ma'am.' The sergeant smiled gratefully and returned to his desk, looking mightily relieved.

Luckily for Bevan, the Fisher case was one which had passed through Nicholson's inbox, requiring his scrutiny in the DCS's capacity as Media Liaison Chief for Police Scotland. He was actually quite cheered to think that Dani might be casting her eyes over the details. He didn't want anything to come back and bite them during the up-coming trial.

'The thing is,' Bevan said on the phone to the Detective Chief Super. 'I need Andy Calder to help me sort through the material. It's the kind of thing he's good at – spotting stuff that another officer might have missed.'

'As opposed to working well with others, you mean,' the DCS chipped in dryly. 'I sent him on that course for a reason.'

'I know that. He's done a couple of days now. Something must have rubbed off.'

Nicholson sighed. 'Okay, call him back. But make good use of the man and for heaven's sake keep Calder on a tight leash, Danielle.'

*

DC Andy Calder arrived at Dani's flat just after breakfast. He wore a casual sweater and dark cords. As the DCI pulled open her front door, the man was sporting a grin which stretched from ear-to-ear.

He stepped eagerly over the threshold. 'I can't thank you enough for getting me off the course, Ma'am. I've experienced some horrors in my time on the force, but nothing compares to that.'

Dani had the files laid out on her kitchen table and a pot of fresh coffee placed close to hand on the counter. 'You're exaggerating, *surely*.'

'I've been less patronised by infant school teachers,' Andy declared. 'The guy running the seminars had swallowed a book full of management clichés. Unfortunately for the rest of us, he kept regurgitating his favourites. I've taken part in more role-plays in the last forty-eight hours than any self-respecting man would ever admit to. At one point, I thought he was going to bring out the Duplo bricks and give us some play time on the mat.'

Bevan couldn't prevent herself from laughing. She'd been on plenty of similar courses in the past. 'When you've reached officer rank, you have to learn to suck it up, Andy. It's the only way to progress.'

Calder gave a theatrical shudder and poured out a cup of coffee. 'Now, can we *please* get on with some proper police work?'

Dani took a seat opposite her colleague, watching

him select a croissant from the basket and start munching it absent-mindedly. Since recovering from a heart-attack a couple of years ago, Andy had completely changed his lifestyle, visiting the gym regularly and laying off the fatty foods. But in recent months, she had noticed him slipping back into some of his old, unhealthy habits. He certainly wasn't the weight he'd once been, but Dani supposed that over time the fear generated by the heart attack had begun to fade and an equilibrium was reached. She hoped for Andy's wife and daughter's sake that he wasn't letting things slide too much.

Andy was sifting through the crime scene photographs. He set down his half-eaten pastry. 'The attacks on the wife and son were incredibly frenzied.'

Dani nodded sombrely. 'Peggy Fisher suffered thirteen stab wounds to the chest. In Callum's case, there were even more – including defensive wounds to his arms and hands. The lad put up one hell of a fight.'

'How tall was the boy?'

'5'5" and of average build for his age. Eric Fisher is 5'11" and physically fit. Callum didn't really ever stand a chance.'

Andy moved the photographs around the table. 'The murder of the little girls is quite different in character. The knife wasn't used. There aren't even any bruises evident where the man held them down under the water. Do you think Fisher killed them first? Did something happen after that to make him really angry?'

'Perhaps the daughters were never the target. His anger may have been focussed purely on Peggy. Perhaps the boy tried to defend his mother and that's what riled Fisher up.'

'How much do you know about domestic homicides, Ma'am?' Andy looked at his boss carefully.

'Only what I've read in the training packs. I've never actually worked one. How about you?'

'When I started out in the western division, we were called out to the aftermath of a fire at a council flat in Greenock. The mother and three kids had died of smoke inhalation. The father claimed he was kipping on a mate's sofa and fast asleep when it happened. His wife had kicked him out the week before. It didn't take us long to realise he'd set fire to the place – murdering his own wife and children. The guy's still banged up in Barlinnie.'

'That is the typical pattern though, isn't it? The husband has become estranged from his family and fears losing contact with the kids. All of his anger and frustration become channelled on his ex-partner. The children are simply innocent pawns in the conflict between their mum and dad.'

'Were Fisher and his wife having problems?'

'According to Sally Irving-Bryant, Eric Fisher claims they had the perfect marriage.' Dani raised her eyebrows and took a sip of coffee.

'What did the family and friends have to say on the matter? Did eastern have any record of domestic violence at the address?'

'The police didn't find any evidence of Fisher being violent towards his family, but a couple of Peggy's friends said that Eric could be very possessive. The woman always had to run it by her husband before she made plans. If they did go out for drinks in Edinburgh, Peggy would be nervous all night – always checking her phone.'

'But she had the wee girls. Folk might say the same about Carol. She doesn't actually like going out in the evening any more, she's forever calling to make sure Amy's okay. I'd take offence if I didn't know it was natural.'

'Fair point.' Dani sat back in her seat. 'Eric Fisher was definitely living at home with his family at the time he killed them. It's unusual in a case of domestic homicide.'

'But the murders took place on a Sunday, which is typical in family annihilation,' Andy added. 'It's the time when the father has greatest access to the children. If he's under pressure at work, the weekend coming to a close could trigger his desire to end the cycle.'

'I want to look more closely at Fisher's finances. There are some details here in these files, but not enough to provide me with the full picture. I think our next move should be to speak with Phil's contact on the original investigating team.'

Andy drained his cup. 'Aye, Ma'am. That's a good idea.'

Chapter 4

Dani Bevan stood on the pavement with DI Mike Tait and gazed across the quiet road at the Fishers' property.

'It's empty, so we can go inside.' Mike led the way to the front door. It was a typical, pebble-dashed council property with relatively newly fitted double-glazing at the windows.

Most of the flooring in the hallway had been ripped up. The place was stone cold. 'Why have the local authority not redecorated?' Dani stepped carefully through the passageway, heading towards the kitchen.

'Fisher's lawyers insisted it remain a crime scene until they completed their investigations,' Mike explained. 'Mind you, I can't see anyone wanting to live here now.' He ran a hand through his untidy grey hair.

'You'd be surprised,' Dani muttered under her breath. She looked down at the dark, puddled stain on the linoleum.

'It's amazing that the guy survived, considering the amount of blood that pumped out of him.'

'Did you attend the scene?'

Tait nodded grimly. 'It's the worst I've ever witnessed.'

'And Eric Fisher was the only one still alive when the neighbour found them?'

'Yes. Peggy had been dead for at least an hour before we arrived. The boy, maybe twenty minutes less.'

'What about the two little girls?' Dani watched his face closely, noting the shadow which passed across his features.

'The pathologist reckoned that the twins were the first to die. He just held their heads under the water until they stopped breathing.' Tait balled his hands into fists and released them again. 'We should never have called an ambulance for the bastard. It would have saved the taxpayer a whole load of money for this farce of a trial if we hadn't.'

Dani pretended she didn't hear his last comment. 'The times of death don't match with Eric Fisher's claims. He says that the girls were alive when he was bundled into the airing cupboard.'

Tait raised his eyebrows incredulously, as if she were a fool to even be considering this possibility. 'We found no forensic traces of Fisher in that cupboard.'

'Were the tests carried out straight after the murders?'

The DI shifted from one foot to the other. 'No. We sent the white coats in again after Fisher provided his new statement. It was maybe three weeks later.'

Dani nodded, making no comment on this. 'Were the neighbours re-questioned about the possibility of an intruder hanging around the property on the day the murders took place?'

Tait puffed himself up, seeming more confident on this topic. 'Yes, we did a house-to-house on this street and the one which backs onto it at the rear. No one saw a thing, just like when we asked them the first time.'

Bevan spent another ten minutes inspecting the house before allowing DI Tait to drive her back to the station.

The investigation into the deaths of the Fishers had operated out of the headquarters of the City and Borders Police on Fettes Avenue in Edinburgh. Bevan was introduced to the SIO of the case, DCI

Annie Carmichael. Dani's opposite number was tall, with a bob of ash-blond hair and strikingly green eyes. The woman was well into her forties and had a formidable presence. Bevan took a soft seat in Carmichael's office, waiting for her to summon the details of the case onto her computer screen.

'So, Ms Sally Irving-Bryant has been in contact with you?' Annie directed her piercing gaze at Dani.

'Aye, she's an old contact of mine and wanted some advice.'

'Well, the advice I would give her is to get Eric Fisher to plead guilty and end this circus right now. Peggy Fisher's family have suffered enough already.'

'But the main reason I'm here is because DCS Nicholson wants to know we've covered our arses.'

Annie chuckled.

'What if there's actually some element of truth in Eric's claims?' Dani braced herself for the woman's tirade but was surprised to see a careworn smile creep across Annie Carmichael's face.

'We took them very seriously, DCI Bevan. The press are crawling all over this case, so we could hardly not do so.' Annie tilted her screen so that Dani could see the information she was referring to. 'Forensics didn't find a single trace of another individual in that house. We could only place the five family members and the neighbour who found them in that property on the day they died. Eric Fisher's account is riddled with contradictions, particularly in relation to the order of the events. His version simply doesn't match the *post mortem* and crime scene evidence we have. I intend to put that point very clearly to the court at his trial.'

'What about a *motive*, Annie? Don't underestimate Sally Irving-Bryant, she's a brilliant advocate. Sally will make it crystal clear to the courtroom that Fisher didn't have any real motive to kill his family. The jury always wants to be able to understand *why*.'

The Detective Chief Inspector sat back in her seat and folded her arms across her chest. 'Have you heard about the use of 'psychological autopsies'?'

Dani shook her head.

'There's an MP in England who's demanding that they should be performed in every UK incidence of family annihilation. We had a lady from the NYPD, who'd trained at Quantico, over here on the team with us for a couple of weeks. She performed a psychological autopsy on Eric Fisher and his extended family. This involved questioning him and all his closest relatives and friends. A full history of the man was created.' Annie reached for a paper file on a shelf behind her and dropped it on the desk between them. 'This is it. I received it from the US on Monday. We've already disclosed it to Fisher's defence team, but it would seem that Sally Irving-Bryant hasn't shared the juiciest details with you.'

Bevan narrowed her eyes. 'Can I read it?'

'Yes. But it remains strictly confidential. This evidence is crucial to the prosecution case.'

'Of course. If Eric Fisher is guilty of this crime, I'm as keen as you are to see him go down for it.'

Chapter 5

The Pentland Hotel was situated in Edinburgh's Old Town and Dani's room possessed a view of Holyrood Palace. The impressive baroque building, once the permanent residence of the Scottish monarchy, was not grabbing the detective's attention. Instead, she was sitting cross-legged on the double bed, with the contents of Annie Carmichael's file spread out across the quilt in front of her.

Eric John Fisher was born at the Edinburgh Royal Infirmary in April 1972. The family lived in Leith and Eric's father worked at Henry Robb's shipyard, losing his job when the yard closed in the early eighties. Leonard Fisher was never in full-time employment again until his death ten years ago. Eric left school at 16 to start earning money for the family. As a young lad, he'd taken an apprenticeship in joinery and worked for various building firms until starting up his own business at the age of 25.

Not long after this, Eric met Peggy Wheelan at a nightclub in Edinburgh. She was on a weekend away with a group of pals, but lived with her parents in Dalkeith. They began a relationship, finally setting up home together, near to Peggy's family, in 2001.

Dani looked up from the notes, gazing around at the dark furnishings of her mock gothic bedroom. Peggy had only been 18 years old when she met Eric Fisher. They'd dated for over four years before moving in together as a couple. The detective thought this was unusual. She turned back to the file. Callum was born in 2002. The couple had married in 2009 and had the twins in 2011.

Peggy Fisher was 35 years old when she died, younger than Dani was. Bevan looked closely at a photograph from their wedding day. Peggy wore her dyed blond hair in a twist on top of her head and her make-up was heavily applied. Despite this, it was obvious the woman had been extremely pretty. Eric was dressed in a grey morning suit, with a hand placed around his wife's narrow waist. His hair was naturally dark and his face tanned and handsome. Bevan took a sip from the mug of sugary tea she'd placed on the bedside table. Both Peggy's parents were still alive and lived just a few streets away from the house in which their daughter was killed.

Peggy's sister was questioned extensively by Janette Morrow, the American consultant to City and Borders Police. According to her, Eric Fisher was possessive and manipulative. Gracie Wheelan was with her sister when she first met Fisher at the club in Edinburgh. Even back then she'd not taken to him, claiming the man was very aware of his considerable good-looks and a charmer with the ladies.

Gracie was convinced he'd had a number of other girlfriends in the city before finally settling down with Peggy. Morrow had asked if any of these girlfriends were still on the scene at the time of the murders. The sister was forced to admit she didn't think so.

Dani shook her head, flicking through the many pages of interview transcripts. There was plenty of evidence here about Eric, provided by Peggy's friends and family, most of it uncomplimentary but without solid evidence to back it up.

Bevan would expect that, particularly in the aftermath of a crime in which the press had already decided Fisher was guilty. What Dani wanted to see more of was information about *Peggy's* life and background. It was her and the children who were the victims of this terrible atrocity. As a detective, she needed to know more about *them.* If *Peggy* had a boyfriend then that would provide a much clearer motive for her murder than if Eric Fisher had been the one playing the field.

The phone by Dani's side began to buzz. It was a text message from Sally. They'd arranged to meet at a bar in the Grassmarket in half an hour. The lawyer was confirming she'd be there. Bevan was about to leave the file for the time-being and take a quick shower when a piece of paper amongst the pile caught her attention. It was a hospital letter.

Dani snatched the document up. The letter was dated three months before the murders and appeared to contain the results of a paternity test. Bevan gawped at the words printed on the sheet for several minutes before rushing into the bathroom to get ready for her appointment.

*

It was still early and the bar was quiet. Dani ordered a glass of red wine and took a table by the window, waiting for her companion to arrive. She gazed out at the darkening street. A noisy group of students were heading for the Salsa bar, a place advertising cheap deals on pitchers of Sangria and bottles of Spanish lager. Dani saw Sally approach, her long stride un-curtailed by the high heels she wore. The lawyer pushed through the door, lowering the mobile phone held to her ear when she spotted Bevan. She pointed in the direction of the bar to indicate she'd get a drink before joining her.

When Sally reached the table, with a glass of gin and tonic in hand, the phone was safely tucked away in her bag. 'Thanks so much for meeting me,' she began, crossing one elegant leg over the other. Wasting no time she added, 'have you had a chance to review any of the case notes?'

'I have. You didn't tell me everything Sally.'

The woman tipped her head to one side innocently. 'What do you mean?'

'DCI Carmichael gave me a copy of the 'psychological autopsy' file this morning.'

'Ah, I see. Well, my chambers didn't receive that information until a few days ago. My assistant is still going through it all.' Sally put the stubby glass to her mouth, leaving a crimson imprint from her painted lips along the rim.

'But you know about the hospital letter?'

The lawyer nodded. 'There's an explanation for that.'

'*Really*?' Dani laid her palms flat on the table. 'I'd love to hear it.'

Sally took a healthy swig. 'Eric says that he and Peggy had an argument a few months before his wife's death. According to him, it started out as nothing serious. Peggy was accusing Eric of not doing enough to help out with the twins. She said he was always eager to take Callum to the footie or the cinema but it was the little girls that really required the hard work. Peggy became upset and tearful. In the heat of the moment, she said that he shouldn't bother in future because the twins weren't even his.'

'Why would she say that?'

'Eric doesn't really know which is why it continued to prey on his mind. As soon as the words were out Peggy retracted them, claiming she'd only said it to get back at him. But Eric found himself thinking about it all the time. Eventually, he persuaded Peggy to allow him and the girls to take a paternity test.'

'And the results showed that the twins were his,' Dani chipped in.

'Yes. Eric said that was the end of it.'

Bevan leant forward. 'But it hardly indicates that the Fishers had the happiest of marriages, does it?'

Sally sighed. 'No. Although Eric insists that they didn't argue often, this disagreement was unusual.'

'Neither of us has children, but I still don't reckon that's the kind of thing you'd normally say in the heat of an argument, do you?' Dani finished off her wine.

'I'm not sure. Perhaps if Peggy was exhausted looking after the twins and particularly frustrated with her husband, she might want to say something that was intended to really wound him.'

'But once the words were out, Eric began to brood on them. They could have been circling around in his head for months before he persuaded Peggy to agree to the paternity test. During that time he'd been suspecting his wife of all sorts. This could be the psychological trigger for the murders that the prosecution have been looking for.'

Sally nodded dejectedly. 'Yes, it could well be.'

Dani's expression softened. 'But three months before the killing of his wife and children, Eric Fisher *did* discover that the twins were actually his. The man's fears were put to rest. The whole episode says more about Peggy than it does about her husband.'

'How do you mean?'

Bevan shuffled forward. 'I've been reading through the files very carefully. What has struck me is how little information there is about Peggy. My suspicion is that she was the primary victim in this attack. In the course of a typical murder investigation, *her* life would be examined inside and out. I'm not convinced that City and Borders have done that thoroughly enough. If I were you, that's where I'd focus my attentions.'

Sally narrowed her eyes thoughtfully, before lifting the tumbler to toast her companion. 'Thanks for the advice. I'll be sure to do that.'

Chapter 6

Louise Keene collapsed into an armchair in the front room of her parents' home in Falkirk. She'd just opened the patio doors and allowed her two young sons to race out into the garden to find the football.

'I'll make us a pot of tea,' her mother called in from the kitchen.

'Great, that's just what I need.' Louise rested her head on a cushion and closed her eyes for a moment, reflecting on their busy day spent sightseeing in Edinburgh. She couldn't imagine how her boys had so much energy left. Louise felt a hand gently squeeze her arm, opening her eyes again to see Joy Hutchison place a cup of tea on the table beside her daughter. 'Thanks Mum.'

Joy gazed out at her grandsons tearing around the lawn, making no move to go and close the doors. 'It's rather mild today. Spring is definitely coming.'

Louise shifted herself up and lifted the cup to her lips. 'Where's Dad?'

'Your father is waiting in with Rita across the road. She's having someone replace her locks today. He doesn't think she should be left alone until the job's been done.'

Louise turned her large brown eyes towards her mother, a look of concern on her attractive face. 'It's a bit of a worry, all these burglaries taking place on your estate - especially after what happened to Dad before.'

'That was another matter entirely. Richard

Erskine is in prison now and he won't be released during our lifetime.' Joy gripped her mug resolutely, adding, 'I'm *more* concerned that Bill will start trying to find out who is responsible for these break-ins. You know what your father's like.'

Louise nodded sagely, she certainly did. Ever since her older brother had died at a tragically young age, her Dad had tried to get over it by fixing every injustice he came across. Sometimes, this one-man crusade could be downright dangerous.

Jamie Keene came dashing in from the garden, depositing a trail of muddy prints on the beige carpet. 'Is tea ready yet?'

'Give us a chance!' His mother laughed.

Joy sprang to her feet. 'It'll be ready in twenty minutes dear,' she replied to the lad's rapidly retreating form. 'You sit there and finish your drink Louise. I'll rustle something up for the boys.'

*

Bill Hutchison was home in time for dinner. He hung his jacket up in the hallway and went straight into the kitchen, where Joy was stirring a pot on the stove. 'Louise is upstairs bathing the boys. How is Rita?'

'Still a bit shaken, but relieved that the new locks are in. I helped her to get the place tidied up. That's why I'm late.' Bill lowered himself into a chair at the table. 'They didn't take much, just a few items of jewellery – along with the television set, of course.'

'It's a shame Rita hadn't still got that big heavy one. They'd have had a struggle shifting that beast out unnoticed.'

'Aye, these slim-line models are easy pickings. Rita knows it was lucky she was at her daughter's house when it happened. There wasn't actually too much damage done. Her photographs were all still in place – including the big one of Christopher. Imagine how upset she'd have been if it had got broken, or the print torn?'

'Goodness, I hadn't thought of that.' Joy turned around and looked at her husband.

'Thought of what?' Louise breezed into the room, picking up the half full wine glass she'd left on the counter and taking a healthy swig.

'That the burglars may have damaged the photograph of Rita McCulloch's grandson – the chap who was killed out in Afghanistan,' Bill explained.

His daughter tutted loudly and shook her head. 'How awful, to steal the property of a pensioner.'

'It makes me wonder if I shouldn't put away that photograph of Neil,' Joy suddenly said. 'It's the only copy we've got. I'd hate for something to happen to it.'

'I could take it back to Glenrothes with me and have more copies made from it. Fergus has got a friend who's a real whizz at that sort of thing. We should have done it years ago.'

'Yes please darling, that's a great idea.' Joy returned to dishing up the food, seeming more contented.

Bill remained quiet until they were all seated at the dining table and tucking into their meal. 'I wonder why the burglars left Christopher's picture alone. The frame is gold-plated. I might have thought they'd have taken it. They certainly targeted all the gold jewellery on Rita's dressing table. It would have fetched a few bob for scrap.'

'Perhaps they had a heart after all and realised it must be of sentimental value. It's got pride of place on her mantelpiece.' Joy took a sip from her glass of Cotês du Rhone.

'Not many burglars have a conscience,' Louise

muttered cynically.

'You're right Louise,' Bill added with feeling. 'They don't. But perhaps they were displaying a sentimentality of a different kind.' He picked up his glass and swirled the liquid around so that it nearly touched the rim. 'In the photo, Chris is wearing his full dress uniform. Maybe it was *that* fact which made the intruder hesitate to disturb it.'

'You think there might be a military connection to these break-ins?' Louise looked interested.

'It's certainly possible,' her father replied.

'Well, that's a matter for the police,' Joy cut in firmly, determined to change the subject. 'Now, what does everyone want for dessert?'

Chapter 7

When DCI Bevan returned to her hotel room she discovered another text message on her phone. Sally had informed her, just as they were parting ways outside the bar, that her brother was back living in Edinburgh. She'd promised to forward his details.

Dani had met James Irving on a previous case. His friend had been murdered during a walking holiday in Loch Lomond. At the time, James was practising as a solicitor down in London. Sally explained that their mother had been ill recently and this prompted her younger brother to make the move back to Scotland. Dani wasn't surprised. The man had lost his two best mates. There was nothing much left for him in London any longer. She glanced at the details, saving them to her address book. It appeared that James now had a flat in Marchmont.

The detective kicked off her shoes and lay down on the bedclothes, staring up at the swirling patterns in the plaster work covering the high ceiling. She decided to call the reception desk and book in for another couple of nights. It seemed as if Bevan would have a fair few visits to make whilst she was through in the east and wanted to start first thing in the morning.

*

Andy Calder met his boss on the southside of Edinburgh. She climbed into the passenger seat of his car and instructed her DC to drive them to Dalkeith. Dani filled her partner in on what she'd learned so far about the Fisher case. Calder listened in silence, apparently concentrating all his attentions on the wonders of the eastbound A7.

'So, Fisher is in his early forties with a working class background. The guy has a limited education and now runs his own building repair business. His wife is a good few years younger than him and very attractive,' Andy finally summarised. 'His background fits perfectly with a typical perpetrator of domestic homicide. I found out some fresh information about his finances back in Glasgow. Eric Fisher's cash flow had all but dried up in the months before the murders. A long running contract he'd held with the local authority hadn't been renewed. I'd say he's got the textbook profile to be the killer.'

Dani nodded. 'It looks that way. If Eric was feeling under pressure at work then Peggy certainly didn't help matters by suggesting to her husband that he wasn't the father of their children.'

Andy furrowed his brow. 'Why would she say something like that when it wasn't true?' He glanced across at his boss and caught her eye, 'unless she wasn't totally sure herself. It might have come as a surprise to her when those tests came back showing that Eric really was the dad. It might purely have been a lucky break for the woman.'

Bevan shifted around in her seat. 'And if Eric suspected that too, then the result wouldn't have taken away his fear that Peggy had been unfaithful.'

They pulled up outside a neat semi-detached property a few streets away from the Fishers' place. Dani and Andy approached the front door and pushed the bell.

A man in his late fifties opened up. Dani introduced herself, explaining that she was the person who'd spoken to him earlier on the phone. He couldn't quite manage a smile but muttered the necessary pleasantries in a dull monotone. Rob Wheelan led them into a tidy front room. Andy perched on a small upright sofa which made him look like a giant.

'Can I make you a brew?' The man asked.

'I'll come and help you,' Dani replied, thinking it might be a good idea for Mr Wheelan to busy himself with a task. When they entered the bright kitchen extension she said, 'is your wife at home?'

Rob sighed heavily. 'Pat's having a lie down. I'll fetch her if you really want?'

Dani shook her head gently. 'There's no need. We've only got a couple of questions for you. We want to ensure that the case is watertight when it comes to trial.'

The cups clattered together and one fell onto its side as Peggy's father brought the china clumsily out of a cupboard. Dani set them upright again, proceeding to drop teabags into each one.

'Thank you,' he said. 'I'm jittery at the thought of the trial. Pat and I are very worried about it. We don't know quite what to expect.'

Dani knew that with Fisher pleading not guilty the trial would be an ordeal for the Wheelans. Every single detail of their daughter and grandchildren's lives would be dredged up by the defence. Sally Irving-Bryant pulled no punches. 'When my mother died, under difficult circumstances, my dad never went to the inquest. I was too young to go anyway. He used that as a reason to stay at home. In reality, he simply couldn't bear to hear all the terrible details. He knew it wouldn't change anything.'

Rob looked at her in surprise. 'I thought we *had* to go. I didn't think we had a choice.'

Dani rested her hand on his arm. 'Of course you

have a choice. It's about you and your wife now.'

Tears sprang to the man's eyes. 'It's going to sound awful, but we've been trying to focus our attention on our other daughters – Gracie has two little ones and so has Liz. We want to be strong for them. My wife and I want to get past this so we can see them grow up.'

'You shouldn't be ashamed to think like that. It's perfectly natural and the only way through this nightmare.'

Dani took over making the teas and found a tray to carry them into the lounge. When the pair entered, Andy was examining the photographs on the window sill. He swiftly returned to his seat.

Once Mr Wheelan was settled into an armchair with his drink Dani said, 'Rob, if it isn't too painful, could you tell us a little about Peggy?'

'Yes. I'd like that. Since this whole thing happened no one has really been interested in our daughter. All the questions have been about Eric. What would you like to know?'

'Just tell us what Peggy was like as a person – what were her interests and passions?'

Rob's lower lip began to tremble again but he took a deep breath and composed himself. 'Peggy always loved dancing and singing when she was wee. She was such a pretty girl and for a while we thought Peggy might choose to go to stage school. She wasn't quite tall enough for modelling. She studied for her Highers and got a decent set of grades. It was the humanities subjects that she enjoyed. Before Peggy had the twins, she was working at the Arts Centre in the town, doing the admin and answering phones, but she'd also started to get involved with the classes. Then she fell pregnant and the job stopped when the girls came along.' Rob swallowed back a sob. 'I suppose Peggy might have gone off to college if she hadn't met Eric, but it was never part of the plan. It's not like their relationship held her back, which is what the police inspector was suggesting. Peggy wanted to get married and have children. She was upset that it took them so long to have more kiddies after Callum. Then two came along – that's the way it goes sometimes, isn't it?'

Dani nodded and smiled, not wishing to interrupt his flow.

'When the girls started at pre-school, Peggy got a job at the travel agency in town. She really enjoyed it, especially meeting all the clients. Peggy was a really sociable lass. But it's tough with twins. I reckon Eric did his best to help but he'd had a lot of work on. The man needed to pay the bills – that's what I told our Peggy when she complained about him being away from home so much.'

'So Eric Fisher had a lot of building jobs on in the weeks leading up to the tragedy?' Andy shuffled forward a fraction.

Rob nodded. 'There's a new estate just been built over near Eskbank. Eric was fitting them out – with new kitchens and the like. There are getting on for two hundred houses going up. Eric was really busy. He'd even taken on a young lad to help him.'

'You don't happen to know the name of this lad, do you?' Andy asked casually.

Rob screwed up his face. 'He's the son of one of Eric's mates. I can't quite recall his name – Carl, maybe?'

'That's fine. We can check it out for ourselves,' Andy replied.

Dani placed her cup carefully on the coffee table. 'Why do you think Eric might have killed your daughter?'

Rob blinked his eyes vigorously. 'I don't know.

Gracie keeps telling us that it was bound to happen and we should have taken action sooner. She says Eric was too possessive of Peggy. But Pat and I didn't see it that way. To us, Eric was an old-fashioned kind of husband. He didn't want Peggy tottering about the town at night in short skirts and high heels with her mates. Gracie's Keith doesn't appear to mind in the slightest where she goes and what state she's in when she comes back. I wouldn't have let my Pat go out that way and have other blokes ogling her. Eric was a working man – a decent father. None of this makes any sense to me.' Rob shook his head sadly.

'Thank you so much for your time Mr Wheelan.' Dani put the empty cups back on the tray and carried them into the kitchen, intending to wash up the dirty crockery before they left.

Chapter 8

'Eric must have been working cash-in-hand on those new builds,' Andy commented. The detectives had stopped for lunch in a café on the outskirts of Dalkeith. 'There was no evidence of the money having been deposited into his bank account or being reported to the Revenue.'

'So where is the cash now?' Dani bit into her bacon sandwich, the warm rasher making the sliced bread soggy and difficult to handle. 'I wonder if Fisher told Sally Irving-Bryant about his illegal working practices.'

'Was there any mention in the police files of this young lad Fisher was employing?'

'No, I don't recall reading anything about him. It would be worth having a talk with the boy though, to see how lucrative the job was. If Eric had a good income stream after all, it undermines our theory that economic strain had pushed him to commit the murders.'

'Aye, but the lad's not going to come forward willingly, not if the arrangement wasn't legit.'

'But this is a multiple murder inquiry. Surely the boy would know we're not interested in his petty tax evasion.' Dani shook her head in frustration. 'Why didn't the original investigating team work this lead more rigorously?'

'Maybe they didn't ask the right questions in the first place. Rob Wheelan really opened up to you. He's even asked if he can contact you before the trial starts, to give them some advice on how to proceed.'

Bevan shrugged this off. 'Possibly, but the man is a cooperative witness, he certainly doesn't appear to be biased against his son-in-law. The SIO should have got more out of the Wheelans at the time they were first interviewed. Their laxness may have created the chance of a 'not guilty' verdict, or the grounds for a later appeal. DCS Nicholson won't be happy.'

Andy wiped the remaining traces of tomato ketchup from his lips with a paper napkin. 'It wasn't what the team wanted to hear. They had Eric firmly in the frame. The questions they asked would have followed on from that assumption. He probably *is* guilty you know.'

'*Probably* isn't good enough in a court of law. That's the equivalent of a 'not proven' verdict.' Dani shook another miniature packet of sugar into her tea. 'I reckon it would be worth going to visit this building site in Eskbank and see what the folk there remember.'

'Aye,' Andy responded brightly. 'That's a good plan.'

*

Eskbank was an upmarket suburb on the western edge of Dalkeith. The River View Estate looked close to completion. Narrow roads filled with almost identically designed executive new-builds spread out before the detectives, ending at tall fences beyond which lay nothing but wasteland. Andy parked in front of the show home and sales office.

A man with a closely shaven head, sporting a shiny suit showed them into an office which smelt of new carpet. 'What can I do for you?' He asked warily, gesturing for the police officers to take a seat.

Dani placed a photograph of Eric Fisher on the desk between them. 'Is it correct that this man did some building work for you from the November of

2013 up until the summer of last year?'

The man nodded. 'Aye, Eric did the internal carpentry and fitted the kitchens. He had all the correct qualifications and insurance.'

'How was he paid?' Andy enquired bluntly.

The man shifted about in his seat. 'Mr Fisher preferred to be paid in cash. Our finance officer said this wasn't a problem. It was up to our contractors to declare their own taxable earnings. It wasn't our responsibility.'

'Were you questioned by the police when Eric Fisher was arrested for the murder of his family last year?'

He shook his head. 'I heard about it obviously. I assumed it must have been some kind of domestic dispute. We were trying to sell the final few plots here when the story broke. To be honest, we weren't keen at the time to have our association with Fisher made public.'

'So you never approached the police yourself, to inform them that Fisher had been working for you?'

'No.' The man had the good grace to look embarrassed.

'Do you recall Fisher having any associates working alongside him?' Andy fixed the salesman with a steely glare.

'There was a young lad, looked about sixteen years old. He did all the shifting and carrying.'

'What was his name?' Dani asked.

'I think it was Craig.'

'Could you provide us with a description of this boy?' Andy pressed, with barely contained irritation.

'Of course, anything I can do to help.'

*

'All of Eric Fisher's friends and family will have to be

re-interviewed to determine who this lad is.' Dani stared out at the metal grey clouds and sighed. 'DCI Carmichael is going to be mightily pissed off.'

'What? Because we've done their job for them?'

'This evidence may prove to be irrelevant to the question of Fisher's guilt.'

'But it proves the investigation wasn't thorough enough, which is what your lawyer friend suspected from the start. Are you going to tell her about this new evidence?'   .

Dani winced, her loyalties torn between her colleagues on the police force and the desire for Eric Fisher to receive a fair trial. 'Once we've passed the information to City and Borders, they are required to disclose it to the defence team.' She lowered her voice. 'But I'm inclined to tell Sally everything now, then she'd have time to question Eric properly about it and mount a decent case. I just keep recalling the last time I withheld evidence because I *thought* it was for the greater good. I don't have the right to do that. The jury should be made aware of absolutely everything, even if it means a guilty man walks free.'

'You shouldn't let what happened with Karlsen affect your judgement, Ma'am. The guy was a manipulator and a crook.'

'I know that. But I can at least learn some lessons from the whole sorry episode.'

Andy said no more and drove them in silence back to Edinburgh.

Chapter 9

This meeting had the potential to be awkward for the DCI. Dani Bevan hadn't seen James Irving for over a year, not since she'd investigated the Ardyle case. Back then, it looked as if their friendship might develop into something more. But it never did.

They met for a coffee in an incredibly ornate café just outside the walls of Edinburgh Castle. Dani was surprised to see that James was dressed casually, in a red polo shirt and jeans. The last time she'd set eyes on him he'd been lying in a hospital bed at the Infirmary, his face badly bruised. The man looked entirely recovered. His handsome face was now lightly tanned and his expression contented.

'Wow, you must get a lot more sun here in the east than we do.' Dani greeted him warmly, depositing a kiss on his cheek.

James cracked a wide smile. 'I've just got back from a ski trip to France. It was sunny, but bloody cold.'

Dani sat down at the table, ordering a cappuccino and some pastries. 'Did Sally tell you why I'm here in Edinburgh?'

He nodded. 'I'm never seen my sister so shaken up by a brief. Sally is usually the epitome of professional detachment. To be honest, I think this Fisher guy freaks her out.'

'I haven't met him yet, only seen the mug shots and read the testimonies.'

Knowing they wouldn't be able to discuss the details any further, Irving changed the subject. 'I suppose Sally informed you that I've moved back to the motherland on a permanent basis?'

'Yes. How is your mum now?' Dani smiled at the waitress as she set down her order.

'Much better thanks. It wasn't anything serious, but these things make you reassess life a bit. Without Jo and Amit, London felt pretty empty.' James sipped his coffee. Dani thought his expression was philosophical. 'How's your American friend?' He suddenly added.

The question took Bevan by surprise. 'Actually, I've not seen him for a while. The distance wasn't really working for us.' Dani felt her cheeks burn.

'I see.' James placed his cup carefully into its saucer, keeping his eyes fixed on the pattern made by the drips of coffee staining the sides. 'I was skiing with a girlfriend of mine this week. We've been seeing each other for several months. This was the first time we'd been away together. Isn't it odd that when I returned there was a message from you on my answer machine?' He slowly raised his gaze.

'Shit. My timing's always been bloody awful.'

Fortunately, James saw the funny side. 'Well, we did say we wanted to remain friends. This is probably our chance.'

'I'd like that very much. I'm learning to appreciate the truly decent people I've got in my life right now. I've not always been the best at doing that in the past. If I didn't treat you very well when we met before, I'm sorry.'

James looked genuinely surprised. 'No apology required.' He narrowed his dark eyes. 'Is everything okay, Dani?'

'Sure, it's fine. We should definitely keep in touch this time though, that's all.'

*

Joy Hutchison was smiling as she laid out their best china tea-set on a tray. She filled the pot and placed it in the centre, carrying the whole thing out to the living room, where their unexpected guest was making herself comfortable on one of the armchairs.

'I could do us all a round of sandwiches whilst I'm at it?' The woman happily declared.

'No Joy, this is absolutely fine for me, thank you.' DCI Bevan leant forward to pour out a cupful.

'To what do we owe this pleasure?' Bill asked with a grin, pleased to see his old friend again.

'I'm still supposed to be on leave, actually. I went to Colonsay for a week to stay with Dad, but now I'm looking into a cold case for a colleague. It brought me to Edinburgh.'

'Well, I'm very glad it did. Louise and the boys have only just returned to Glenrothes. We've had a houseful ourselves these past few days.'

'Are the family keeping well?' Dani put the dainty cup to her lips, savouring the refreshingly aromatic scent of the tea.

'The boys are full of beans, as always,' Joy supplied. 'But Fergus is working long hours at the moment. Louise fancied a break and some help with the children.'

Dani recalled that Fergus Keene worked for an insurance company. She wondered why his job would require particularly long hours, but then reflected how all companies were putting the squeeze on their employees these days. 'I suppose they must be a handful at that age,' she commented instead.

'Yes, but such a tonic to us.' Joy settled down on the sofa next to her husband.

Bill shuffled forward. 'Have your department heard about this spate of burglaries we've had here in Falkirk?'

Dani shook her head. 'I'm afraid we have enough of those in Glasgow to keep us busy.'

'The most recent was at Rita's place,' Bill explained.

Dani sat up straight in surprise, immediately feeling guilty for being so flippant. She thought about the kind old lady she'd interviewed once. 'Is Rita okay?'

Bill nodded. 'She was at her daughter's house when it happened. It's extremely unsettling, nonetheless. A number of valuable items were stolen but some notable pieces were not. The nature of the items they chose not to disturb led me to believe the burglars may have a military connection of some kind.' He recounted the fact that Christopher's photograph had not been damaged when the house was ransacked.

Dani had learnt to take Bill Hutchison's observations seriously. The man had excellent instincts. 'I'll mention this to the investigating team. It's probably the central division who are handling it. Make sure you keep this place well locked up when you go out.' Dani eyed the couple with concern.

'Don't worry. We had an alarm fitted after the incident with Richard Erskine.' Bill paused before saying, 'is it the Fisher case which brings you to Edinburgh?'

The detective was taken aback, but she also knew there wasn't much that got past Bill. 'Why do you ask that?'

'Because I read in the Scotsman that Sally Irving-Bryant is representing the father at the trial. I've kept a close eye on her career since my unfortunate brush with the woman. I consider her to be a net contributor to the number of dangerous criminals walking the streets of Scotland. But I also recalled that you have a connection to the Irving family.'

Dani sighed heavily. If Bill were twenty years younger she'd snap him up for her team. 'I'm not at liberty to discuss the details, I'm afraid.'

Bill waved his hand in a dismissive gesture. 'Of course, I understand entirely.' He tutted loudly. 'Joy and I read all the details of the incident. What a terrible tragedy it was, the fate of that poor woman and her children. I did wonder, with all these burglaries occurring so soon after the Fishers were murdered, and being so widely reported in the press over here in the east, that the father might decide to use them as part of his defence – to suggest there was an intruder in their house that afternoon, perhaps.

One has a great deal of time to think whilst on remand, I should imagine, and not much else to do except watch television and read the newspapers. With a clever and ruthless lawyer like Ms Irving-Bryant in my employ, I'd be tempted to come up with a similar sort of story myself - something to confuse the jury and inject an element of doubt.'

Dani smiled thinly, thinking there wasn't much she could say to this. Instead, she reached forward and lifted the pot, enquiring if her hosts would like a spot more tea.

Chapter 10

Back at her flat, Dani pulled across the file once again, setting down a glass of red wine on the table next to it. She'd passed on all the information gathered from their trip to Dalkeith both to Sally Irving-Bryant's chambers and the local police.

Although the DCI had done her best to ignore his theory, Bill's comments remained firmly lodged in her mind. It might just be possible that Eric Fisher was playing them all for fools. He would know as well as anyone else that the burden of proof was on the prosecution in a murder trial. All Sally needed to do was ensure that the police couldn't prove beyond reasonable doubt that another man *hadn't* killed Peggy Fisher and her kids. It didn't matter how unlikely the scenario was in reality.

Dani downed a quarter of the glass, feeling frustrated. She'd asked central division to forward her the details of all the burglaries committed in Falkirk and the surrounding towns over the past eighteen months. Bill was right. There *had* been a marked increase in cases of breaking and entering in the area. But none of the crimes reported was overly violent in nature. In one case, a man came home from work early and interrupted the burglary. He was shoved to the floor and received a kick to the ribs before the intruder ran off.

There were certainly no incidences in which knives were used on the householders. The scant number of witness statements simply referred to a tallish young man with an unshaven face and possibly with dark hair. Sometimes, the reports referred to a second intruder too. The descriptions of these men were vague and generic.

The SIO seemed interested in Bill's theory of a military connection. It sounded as if the DI in charge was rapidly running out of ideas of his own.

Bevan finished off her wine and decided to call it a night. As she padded down the hallway to her bedroom, the phone began to ring. Dani was tempted to leave it, but something made her hook up the receiver. 'DCI Bevan.'

'Evening, Ma'am. It's Andy here. Sorry to call you so late. I think you should switch on the TV news. We can discuss it further in the morning.'

'Sure, thanks,' Dani said warily, putting down the phone and heading into the living room. She switched on the set and notched up the volume, mesmerised by the breaking news story playing out on the screen. 'Holy shit,' Dani murmured quietly, dropping onto the sofa and leaning forwards to make sure she caught all of the unpleasant details.

*

Bevan and Calder were in Dundee by lunchtime. Grey clouds hung thick over the city. The DC drove them to the police headquarters on Jute Street. A steely receptionist directed the Glasgow detectives to take a lift to the second floor, where DI Gordon Alexander met the pair.

'Thank you for letting us drop in on your investigation,' DCI Bevan began, after shaking the man's hand. The Detective Inspector was tall and broad, with a thick head of dark hair.

'Not at all,' Alexander replied in a deep, resonant voice. 'I'd appreciate your input.'

The DI led them towards an area divided off with

boards displaying a selection of crime scene photos. There were lists of evidence already gathered scrawled onto flip charts. A small group of detectives looked up as Dani and Andy approached, a couple of them muttering their greetings.

'The victim was called Morna Susan Murphy. She was 37 years old and lived on the Invergowrie Estate, which is situated at the foot of the Law.' Alexander pointed to a non-descript area on a map.

'It was her husband who found her?' Andy put in.

'Aye. Lyle Murphy returned home from his job at the local council at roughly 7pm on the evening before last. The house was in darkness. At first, he thought his wife was out. Then Mr Murphy noticed that the kitchen door had been forced open and the living room ransacked. When he ventured upstairs, he discovered his wife's body in the bedroom.' The DI gestured towards a photograph showing a woman lying on her front on a double bed, the back of her light blouse soaked in blood.

'Do you have the preliminary *post mortem* results yet?' Dani enquired.

'Morna was stabbed eighteen times in the back. We assume she was fleeing her assailant at the time of the attack. The murder weapon was found dumped in the garden. It was a knife from the block in the kitchen. The pathologist thinks the woman died about an hour and a half before her husband discovered the body.'

'So has Mr Murphy got an alibi?' Andy stared closely at a photograph of Lyle and Morna together at what appeared to be a christening. They were a good looking couple.

'Lyle Murphy was in a council meeting when his wife was killed.'

'It doesn't mean he didn't pay someone else to kill Morna,' Dani added. 'Were there any witnesses to the break-in?'

DI Alexander furrowed his brow. 'Not so far. We've questioned all the neighbours. One chap, who lives across the road, saw a dark van parked up on the street that day. He'd not seen it before so was suspicious. He thinks it was gone by six pm. But you know what these modern estates are like – everyone is out at work during the day and the roads are jam-packed with parked cars by late afternoon because the driveways are too small to accommodate all the vehicles. So no one notices a damn thing.'

'Had Morna been at work that day?' Dani gazed at her image. A pretty face framed with long, straight blond hair stared back at the detective. Bevan was immediately put in mind of Peggy Fisher.

'Yes. Morna worked at a hotel in the city centre. She was on the reception desk. Her boss said she left the premises at just after five. By our calculations, the woman would have reached home by half past at the latest.'

'She was killed not long after getting home,' Dani commented. 'I wonder if he was already in the house, waiting.'

Gordon Alexander's face became grim. 'We think that is entirely possible. Whether she disturbed the burglary when she arrived back, or the man had targeted Morna specifically, I'm not sure. There was no sign of sexual assault. But the murder definitely took place in the bedroom. There are contrary indications here.'

'I agree,' Dani declared. 'There's more to this than a simple house-breaking gone awry. I'm certain of that.'

Chapter 11

The two detectives sat side-by-side on a small sofa in the bar area of the budget chain hotel they were staying in. Dani was funding this trip herself.

Andy had been quiet for a while, slowly sipping from his bottle of European lager. Finally, he broke the silence. 'The murder of Morna Murphy was frenzied, just like the knife attacks on Peggy and Callum Fisher.'

'Exactly,' Dani continued. 'It was as if the victims had angered this man in some way.'

'Callum could have riled him up by fighting back.' Andy swigged the last few dregs from the bottle.

'But are there any other similarities in the two cases?' Dani looked directly at her colleague. 'This scenario here in Dundee is a classic burglary. The TV was missing and a significant number of valuables. You'd expect to find anger and aggression exhibited in a situation of domestic homicide – it isn't out of place in the Fisher case.'

'But it's out of place in the Murphy murder,' Andy chipped in, used to this kind of interplay with his boss. 'Unless we're talking about a gang of young burglars off their heads on drugs, then all bets are off. There's no knowing how they might react to somebody coming home and disturbing them in the act.'

Dani nodded. 'Aye, that's right. But the use of the van and the careful fencing of the stolen goods suggest a crime that's more organised and less chaotic than that. It's almost as if when he saw the woman, he lost control of himself.'

'Do you think the attacker knew Morna?'

'It is possible. She worked front of house in the hotel. Morna was blond and attractive. He might have seen her around town even, which means the perpetrator is local to the area.'

'It's worth passing that on to DI Alexander. He seems like a straight down the line kind of guy.' Andy shuffled forward, looking as if he were about to leave, then he turned to address his boss once again. 'Does this murder help Fisher's defence?'

Dani nodded solemnly. 'Definitely. We've got a victim whose age and appearance matches Peggy Fisher's very closely. She was stabbed by a knife taken from the house in a frenzied attack. The husband was clearly not the perpetrator. It was an intruder in their home. The murder of poor Morna Murphy couldn't have come at a better time for Eric Fisher and his team.'

*

Bevan was interested to visit the murder scene, having been to the Fisher's place in Dalkeith. She wanted to find out if anything struck her as similar. Bevan and Calder met Gordon Alexander at the Invergowrie Estate. There was room for both of their cars on the driveway. Dani could immediately see that this was a more upmarket street than the one in which the Fishers had lived.

'When Lyle Murphy came home, he parked on the drive like us and approached the house from the front,' Alexander explained, leading the way to the front door, which was emblazoned with strips of garish police tape. 'It was a breezy evening and the man noticed straight away that the house was cold. He proceeded to the kitchen first.'

They padded through the hallway and took the

first left. The back door had been boarded up, leaving the room dark. 'Did he expect to find his wife in here?' Dani speculated.

'It was seven pm, so Murphy probably thought she'd be cooking his dinner. That's what my wife would be doing,' Andy commented, without any concern that this might sound sexist or unreconstructed. Calder wasn't bothered by that kind of thing.

'Was Morna the domestic type? What did Lyle say about her?' Dani glanced at the DI.

Alexander shrugged his shoulders, obviously unsure why it would matter. 'He said something about being irritated to see that no one was in. He'd had a stressful day and wanted his dinner.'

Dani nodded. 'So it would be unusual for her to be out of the house at that time of the evening. If the burglary was planned, and someone watched the house in the weeks leading up to the break-in, the perpetrator would have been aware of that.'

'Were the Murphys happily married?' Andy asked, whilst they examined the rest of the ground floor. 'What were they – late thirties - why hadn't the couple had children yet?'

'I didn't enquire,' Alexander replied, sounding shirty.

Dani wondered if the detective was married himself. 'It could be important, if the attacker was known to Morna.'

The DCI gazed about the living room. It looked bare and slightly grubby without the myriad of expensive goods which had obviously once been housed in there.

'Murphy reckons they took the television, the stereo system and a games console. There was also a camera sitting out on the sideboard which he believes is gone. An original oil painting hung over the gas fire, there. They had that too.' Alexander tipped his head backwards, so his vision was directed at the ceiling. 'Do you want to take a look upstairs?'

'Yes,' Dani responded with a heavy sigh. 'Go ahead.'

As they climbed the narrow stairwell behind Alexander, Dani observed how bulky the officer appeared within this modern box of a house. She tried to imagine the type of building in which a broadly built man like himself would seem at home. Dani couldn't picture one.

The three of them stopped when they reached the landing. Dani recognised the tell-tale sickly sweet smell of recent death. Gordon allowed the Glasgow detectives to enter the bedroom first. Dani stood only on the trays laid by the forensic team. The thick, pale carpet was stained black by the blood. It was sickeningly reminiscent of the Fishers' kitchen linoleum.

The body had been removed, but the imprint was clearly visible in the pattern made by the blood, which must have seeped from out of the multiple wounds. Dani glanced about the room. It was nicely decorated and tidy. There was no sign of a struggle having taken place in there.

As if Alexander could tell her thoughts he said, 'we think Morna was stabbed first in the doorway. There are blood splatters on the wall just here. She must have collapsed to the floor, which is where the woman received the remainder of the blows inflicted. That's why the carpet is so saturated. Then he shifted her onto the bed. Morna can't have been quite dead by this stage, as she was still bleeding out, according to the pathologist.' The DI appeared to take no pleasure whatsoever in imparting these details.

'So she was *placed* on the bed,' Andy stated with interest. 'Why didn't the attacker just leave her and run?'

Dani straightened up and addressed the Dundee officer. 'I think you should get a profiler in. Get them to take a look at the crime scene photos and the pathologist's report. I believe that this murderer had some kind of connection to Morna Murphy. A good professional profiler could give you a better idea of the type of person you might be looking for. I'll give you the number of the Pitt Street serious crime unit. They'll happily provide you with a list of practitioners.'

Alexander managed a thin smile. 'The advice is greatly appreciated, DCI Bevan. I'll do that. We don't get need of the use of such people very often out here. Thank God.'

Chapter 12

Dani lay absolutely still in her double bed, listening to the bird song and the occasional car passing along her wide street. She didn't do this very often. The DCI still took weekend shifts, even though most officers who were of the same rank as her chose not to. This was because they were married and had children, of course. When Dani had her American boyfriend, Sam Sharpe, over to stay, the time had meant a great deal to her. But they'd called off their relationship several months back, without any great acrimony on either part.

She closed her eyes and allowed her mind to drift to her meeting with James Irving. The memory gave Dani a warm sensation. She'd always found him attractive, but during the Joanna Endicott case Dani couldn't possibly have got involved with him.

Irving had a girlfriend now and their relationship seemed to be getting serious. Ah well, she thought, there was no harm in staying friends with the guy. Dani was just slipping into a rather pleasant daydream in which she and James hooked up again when the front door bell rang.

'Bloody hell,' she muttered bitterly, levering herself up and slipping on a dressing gown. Dani pulled it tightly around her and marched towards the front door, peering irritably through the spy hole. She wrenched it open. '*Andy*? Haven't you got your own sodding family to spend Sunday morning with?'

'Actually, no. Carol's mum has taken her and Amy out shopping. They need to buy outfits for a ruby wedding anniversary or something. I was at a loose end.' Andy breezed past his boss, making a beeline for the kitchen. 'I'll put the kettle on while you get dressed, Ma'am.'

Dani stomped into the bedroom, saying nothing. She emerged ten minutes later having showered and pulled on some jogging bottoms and a Glasgow University sweatshirt. The smell of freshly brewed coffee and the sight of a paper bag full of pastries on the table lifted her spirits markedly.

'Are you still going to the gym up on Great Western Road?' Dani poured them both a cup of coffee and sat down.

'Very subtle, Detective Chief Inspector. Is that your way of enquiring if I'm letting things slide?' Andy was grinning, carrying his mug over to join her. He pointed at the murky, brown liquid. 'This is decaf and I'm limiting myself to one croissant only.'

'Is it actually possible to eat more than one croissant?' Dani smiled too. 'I've just noticed that you aren't quite as obsessive about your fitness regime as you were a few months back. I happen to think that's a good thing.'

'So does Carol. Maybe she's wanting to get me into an early grave, eh?' Andy arched an eyebrow as he bit into his pastry.

Dani didn't want to laugh at this. There were times since Andy's heart attack when his humour could be a little off the mark. If Carol had heard him say that she'd be really upset. 'Carol didn't mind you coming over here this morning, did she?'

'She doesn't think we're having an affair, if that's what you're driving at.' Andy chuckled a little too hard at the idea.

'Thanks a lot. I didn't mean that. It's just that it's Sunday morning and this is work.' Dani sipped her strong coffee.

'The Fisher case interests me,' he replied simply. 'I did some more digging into the details of the Dundee murder from the office yesterday.'

'Oh, aye?'

'I was chatting to Phil about it. He'd seen the reports on the news. Apparently, Phil was at training school with Gordon Alexander.'

'Did he get on well with him?'

'Yeah, I think so. They kept in touch for a few years after qualifying. Only Phil recalled that Alexander's wife and children were killed in a car accident. He thought it must have been about a decade ago.'

'Shit,' Dani exclaimed. 'Poor guy. No wonder he seemed so affected by the murder of Morna Murphy. How did it happen?'

'Phil didn't remember the details, so I looked up the newspaper reports from the time. Gordon's wife – Lydia, was driving their kids to see friends in Perth. They were involved in a multiple pile up – a lorry lost control in icy conditions. The children died at the scene but Lydia was in hospital for a few days before she passed away. Gordon had been on duty that day, so he wasn't with them.' Andy twisted his cup round. 'It's difficult to know how you come back from something like that.'

'By throwing yourself into the job, I expect.' Dani thought about the burly, slightly melancholy man they'd met in Dundee and felt a lump forming in her throat which she quickly swallowed down. 'Did you find out anything else?'

'Lyle Murphy has been thoroughly investigated by Alexander's team. He's well respected on the local council. The guy has been pushing for more affordable housing to be built around Dundee. According to his colleagues, he was becoming frustrated by the obstacles his department have come up against, but it looked like he was slowly making progress. Lyle had no large deposits of cash coming in or out of his bank account in the last two years. The Murphys had no significant debt beyond their mortgage and car loans. It seems as if the husband is clean.'

'What kind of opposition might you come up against if you wanted to build more affordable housing?'

'Local residents objecting to expansion into the countryside, or construction companies trying to whack up prices,' Andy mused. 'Somebody always wants to make a profit out of house building. It's Thatcher's legacy.'

'Eric Fisher was working on that new estate of houses in Dalkeith when his family were killed. I wonder if there's any connection?'

'We can't rule it out, I suppose. What are you thinking – construction firms bunging council members back-handers to flout the planning regs? Although I don't see what that would have to do with an ordinary bloke like Fisher. He was pretty low down the food chain, fitting out the kitchens and stuff.'

Dani nodded slowly. 'But it's another factor that potentially links the two cases, so let's bear it in mind.' She sighed. 'But I don't want to get side-tracked from considering the victims here. Morna and Peggy were very alike in looks and age. That's the pattern I find the most intriguing.'

The DCI's line of discussion was interrupted when there was another knock at the door. This time it was hard and insistent. Dani jogged down the hallway to answer it.

Carol Calder was standing on the step, her pretty mouth set in a grim line. A car was waiting at the kerb with its engine running. 'Hi Dani, is Andy here?'

Dani stepped aside, allowing her DC to move forward.

'Is everything okay sweetheart?' He enquired lightly.

'I was surprised when you weren't at home when we got back. Then I saw your note. Mum and Dad would like to take us *all* out for lunch. You were in the office yesterday, Andy.' These words were delivered through gritted teeth.

Carol looked totally pissed off, especially when her gaze turned towards Dani once again and properly took in her casual appearance and freshly washed hair.

'It's my fault,' the DCI put in swiftly. 'I had a new lead in this case we're examining for the DCS and wanted to run it by Andy. I'm really sorry, Carol.'

Andy re-emerged onto the step with his jacket slung over one arm. 'I'll see you tomorrow, Ma'am,' he said brusquely, following his wife towards the parked car. Not giving his boss a backward glance.

Chapter 13

On this particular visit to Edinburgh, Dani had taken her own small hatchback. James Irving had called to invite her to meet him for lunch. Getting to know the area a little better, the DCI agreed to rendezvous with the lawyer in a restaurant on the newly gentrified waterfront at Leith, a few miles north of the city centre.

James was ten minutes late. Dani got the opportunity to watch him approach along the cobblestones in a tightly fitting dark suit. She herself was dressed smartly, hoping to indulge in some police work whilst she was in the area.

Irving broke into a smile when he saw her. The brief flutter of relief and happiness which passed across his face as he took in her appearance sent a spasm of unexpected longing through Dani's body. As a result, she probably looked a little uncomfortable when he finally reached her table.

'This is a lovely place,' she managed to blurt out.

'Yes, but I was perhaps a bit ambitious with the distance from work. It was a bugger trying to hail a taxi. Sorry I'm late.'

James ordered them a smoked salmon salad each and a bottle of white wine to share.

'Aren't we quite close to your parents' house?' Dani enquired, remembering his father's seventieth birthday party which she'd attended the previous year.

'It's a couple of miles away. I've got no clients booked in for this afternoon. I'll probably drop in on

Mum later.' Irving selected a slice of granary bread from the basket on the table and dipped it in a dark pool of olive oil.

'How is Sally? I should really catch up with her whilst I'm in the city – to see how she got on with the leads Andy and I gave her.'

James screwed up his face. 'I actually think that Sally and Grant have gone away somewhere this week. My sister always likes to clear her head before the start of a major trial. They've flown to one of Grant's holiday cottages up on the Moray Firth.'

Dani suddenly recalled the helicopter trip that Sally had made to Colonsay, picturing the red lettering that she and her dad had discerned across the side of the aircraft as it hovered above them. 'Does Grant own Bryant Construction?' She asked bluntly.

'That's right. He built it up from absolutely nothing, mind you. I'm sure a lot of folk think he inherited the business or something. They specialise in renovating properties in the most picturesque and remote parts of Scotland. That's why Grant got his pilot's licence. My brother-in-law is a useful man to know if you're planning a mini break.' James flashed a smile.

The waitress set down their plates. Dani didn't even glance at the food. She simply lifted her knife and fork and prodded at the salad absent-mindedly.

'Did I say something wrong?' James enquired.

Dani shook her head. 'No, of course not. It's just this domestic homicide case of Sally's.' The detective thought for a moment and then decided it was okay to confide in her friend. 'Calder and I discovered that Eric Fisher was working cash-in-hand on an estate of new builds over in Dalkeith at the time he murdered his family. Then, this break-in at the house in Dundee crops up, with certain similarities to the Fisher case.'

'I saw it on the news. It was awful.'

Dani nodded. 'The husband of the woman who was stabbed by the intruder was an employee of the local council. He'd been campaigning to get more affordable housing constructed on the outskirts of the city. It had earned him some enemies.'

'And I've just mentioned that Sally's husband runs one of the biggest construction firms in the country. You're wondering if there's some kind of link.' James sipped his wine.

'I can't imagine what it could possibly be.'

'Neither can I. Grant's firm doesn't really specialise in building residential estates.'

Dani decided to change the subject. She didn't want to drag James into her professional problems.

The lawyer had most of the wine. Dani stuck to her one glass. After finishing a tiny sliver of lemon cheesecake, adorned with a less than generous scoop of ice-cream, Dani glanced at her watch. 'Would you like a lift somewhere?'

'Actually, if you could drop me at Mum and Dad's that would be great.'

The sun was still shimmering over the Firth of Forth as they left the restaurant. Loosened up by the alcohol, James slipped an arm around Dani's waist, guiding her towards the car. When they reached the passenger door, Irving pulled Dani closer, taking her hand in his. '*Or*, we could go back to my place?'

The DCI allowed their lips to meet, enjoying his urgent kisses and the feel of his body pressing up against hers. Then she pulled back. 'I'm not sure it would be such a good idea. What about your girlfriend?'

Irving's expression became serious. 'I couldn't carry things on with Rachel after I'd seen you again. It wasn't fair.'

Dani rested her hands on his chest, feeling the toned shape of his torso through the thin cotton of his shirt. 'I've only recently come out of this relationship with Sam. I don't trust my judgement right now.' She sighed. 'To be honest with you, I'm worried that it would ruin our friendship if we jumped into bed together. I don't want you to immediately lose interest in me. I'd actually like you to stay in my life.'

James looked as if he'd been slapped in the face. He took a step backwards, keeping hold of her hands. 'God. I'm really sorry, Dani. I have a few glasses of wine and then completely throw myself at you. What an idiot. Look, if you're still okay with having me in your car, why don't we drive to my parents' house liked we planned. If Mum's in, how about you stay for a coffee?'

Bevan nodded cheerfully, unlocking the car doors and striding round to take the driver's seat. 'Great idea. Just show me the way.'

*

When Dani had last seen the Irvings' house, it was decorated for James' father's 70th birthday celebrations. Even without the glitz, their square, stone-built property was still impressive. Linda Irving led them through the wide hallway into the large kitchen-diner where a vaulted, glass panelled ceiling was letting in the afternoon light. They took a seat at the central island.

The petit lady, who sported a neat bob of ash-blond hair, leant in to give her son a kiss on the cheek. 'Oh, James, you reek of alcohol. I hope you've not been into the office like that?'

The man laughed. 'We just had a bottle of wine with lunch. I've been nowhere near my new boss, don't worry.'

'As DCI Bevan was driving, I'll assume you had the lion's share. I'd best make a pot of coffee then.' Linda moved across to the cupboard opposite and began bringing out a set of small espresso cups.

Bevan got up to help. 'Please call me Dani,' she said cheerfully.

Linda gave her a sheepish look. 'I'm sorry about the last time we met. I told you some things I really shouldn't have. James was very cross with me when he found out.'

Dani smiled kindly. 'You should never have to apologise for being honest, Mrs Irving. It was good that I got to know everything about James' relationship with Jo. It helped us to solve the case in the end.'

Linda let out a heavy sigh, appearing mightily relieved. 'I'm pleased to hear you say that. It had preyed on my mind for a while.'

'In a murder investigation, people's first instinct is to protect their loved ones, it's only natural. But if you've nothing to hide then telling the truth is always the best option.' Dani perched back up on the stool next to James.

He turned towards her and replied, 'it doesn't always work out that way though does it? Dad and Sally have been involved in dozens of murder cases. The advice they always give their clients is to reveal as little as possible.'

'That's because many of those men are guilty, darling,' his mother pointed out.

'Not all of them, Mum.' James looked indignant.

'I'm not claiming the system is perfect. But if the police have all the evidence available to them, they usually catch the right man.'

'Do you think that this Fisher chap is the right man?' Linda asked unexpectedly. 'Jim and I have followed the case on the news. Sally isn't allowed to provide us with any of the details, but I know my daughter doesn't like him. I can tell.' She sat down opposite her guests, pushing the freshly filled cups towards them.

'From my point of view,' Dani explained, 'I don't believe the police and prosecution have enough evidence yet to make a judgement one way or the other. Hopefully, there'll be a stronger case before the trial starts. Otherwise, the process won't be in the public interest.'

'I'm on Sally's side in everything, of course,' Linda stated with feeling. 'But the thought of that poor family, slaughtered in their own home, especially those two little girls -' Linda's voice wavered. 'Well, I'm just saying that if the man *is* guilty then I'd quite happily see my daughter lose at the High Court next week.'

Dani nodded silently, lifting the tiny cup to her lips, thinking that she whole-heartedly agreed.

Chapter 14

Annie Carmichael drove a sporty BMW. Not for the first time, the DCI marvelled at how other officers of the same rank as her seemed to possess so much more disposable income. Either she was being seriously underpaid or they were shouldering an enormous amount of debt. Dani suspected the latter.

As they drove through the downmarket estate where the Fishers lived, Dani wished they were in a less conspicuous vehicle. She could already sense net curtains being twitched in a kind of Mexican wave along the street as they crawled past.

'This is it,' Annie declared. 'Number 7.'

Carmichael's team had managed to track down a possible candidate for Eric Fisher's young work mate. It turned out that Fisher's cousin lived a few streets away from the family and had a son by the name of Craig. He was sixteen years old.

Annie ignored the bell and hammered on the front door. It was opened by an overweight woman in her forties who appeared extremely harassed. 'Can I help you?'

Carmichael held up her warrant card. 'We're looking for Craig O'Connor.'

'He's upstairs.' The woman stood back.

The corridor was narrow and the police officers were forced to squeeze against her bulky form. The smell of sweat coming from the woman made Dani wrinkle up her nose. The unpleasant odours only got worse as they climbed the stairs and reached the doorway of what they assumed to be Craig's room.

The lad had on a pair of huge headphones and was resting his feet up against the wall. He nearly jumped out of his skin when he noticed them standing there. The boy swiftly removed the ridiculous headgear. 'What's going on?'

'Are you Craig O'Connor?'

He nodded, swinging his long legs around to rest on the grubby carpet. 'Aye.'

'We're here to question you in connection with the murders of Peggy, Callum, Kyla and Skye Fisher. We can either do it here or at the police station.'

His narrow eyes darted back and forth. 'Can we do it here?'

Cartwright suggested they talk in the kitchen. There was a small circular table in there. Val O'Connor grudgingly put the kettle on.

'Do you know why we're here?' The DCI began menacingly.

Craig examined his dirty fingernails. 'Because I was doing some work for Eric before he was arrested.' He lifted his gaze. 'My da' says I don't need to pay no tax on the money. I didn't earn enough.'

Dani never ceased to be amazed by how clued up people could be about the Inland Revenue System when the rules worked in their favour.

'I'm not interested in your flaming personal tax allowance,' Annie spat out irritably. 'I want to know why you omitted to tell the authorities what Eric Fisher had been up to in the weeks before his wife and children were viciously murdered.'

'I didn't think it'd be relevant.' Craig turned down the corners of his mouth sulkily. 'We were fitting out those new houses up at the River View Estate. I helped him to get the materials from the wholesaler. Eric did all the skilled work – the carpentry and stuff. I did the lifting and carrying. He was paid by the boss and I got a few twenties at the end of each week.'

'What was Eric's mood like in those months you were working alongside him? You probably saw more of the man than anyone else during that period,' Dani asked.

'I dunno. He was just normal.'

'Was Eric good to work for, did you have a joke together?' Dani was determined to persist with this line of questioning.

'Eric used to get annoyed with Craig sometimes,' Val chipped in, 'if he was still in bed when he arrived to pick him up, for instance.'

Dani thought this sounded entirely justified.

Craig shook his head. 'No, Mum's wrong, Eric was a decent boss. He used to show me how to do stuff. He said I should try and get an apprenticeship and learn a proper skill.'

'Did you know Callum Fisher well?' DCI Cartwright asked this question.

The boy shrugged his shoulders. 'Yeah, a bit. We played on the Xbox together if there was a family party. He was younger than me, though. We didn't hang out in town or anything.'

'What about Peggy Fisher?' Dani leant in closer. 'What did you think of her?'

Craig blushed.

Dani immediately wondered why.

'I liked Mrs Fisher. If I stopped by their house after work she'd make us a cup of tea and always offered me a biscuit. Sometimes she and the girls had baked cupcakes. She was nice.'

'You make it sound like you don't get fed properly at home,' Val commented indignantly.

Bevan wished the woman wasn't there. 'How did Eric get on with his wife?'

Craig looked directly at Dani. 'He really loved her. Eric was always talking about how great Peggy looked. He said that most men his age had fat wives who'd totally let themselves go.'

Val choked on her tea.

Dani had to suppress a smile. 'So, they were happy together, in your opinion?'

'Oh aye. I can't believe what happened. The Fishers always seemed like the perfect family. Eric used to sit in the pub looking smug whenever one of his mates chatted up the girls in there. I could tell he was thinking that he had everything he wanted back at home. Do you know what I mean?'

Dani nodded.

'Do you know what Eric did with the money?' Annie Carmichael switched the boy's attention back to her. 'He must have received a lot of cash from working on the new estate.'

'We never talked about it.' Craig started picking absent-mindedly at a piece of dried food welded to the table. 'But it wouldn't have gone into a bank. I'm pretty sure of that much.'

Carmichael stood up abruptly. 'Thank you, Craig. That's all for now.' The DCI led her opposite number along the dingy hallway and out into the daylight, turning only to inform the O'Connors that her department would be in touch.

*

Half an hour later, the detectives were back in DCI Carmichael's office. Annie had ordered them both a strong coffee, claiming she needed to get the taste of stewed tea out of her mouth.

'I think he was lying,' Carmichael declared. 'About not knowing where Eric kept the money he earned from the construction company.'

'Yes, it's possible.'

'If so, it gives Craig a motive for breaking into the Fishers' place - if he knew that the cash was hidden in there somewhere.'

'But why would Craig come to the house on a Sunday afternoon, when he knew the whole family would be at home, including Eric? It doesn't make any sense.'

'Unless Craig had a different motive. The lad was jealous of Eric's 'perfect family'. He was sexually obsessed with Peggy Fisher and decided that if he couldn't have her then no one else would.'

Dani was impressed by Annie's colourful imagination. 'An interesting theory, but Craig just didn't strike me as the type.'

Carmichael smiled. 'Me neither. I don't think that Craig O'Connor is a serious contender for our mysterious intruder. What does intrigue me, though, is what happened to the money. I've got a feeling it's an important part of the puzzle.'

Dani nodded. 'And why has Eric Fisher never mentioned it? If the money has gone then it supports the claim that his wife and children were killed as part of a burglary.'

A uniformed officer arrived with a tray of drinks. Carmichael busied herself pouring them each out a cup.

Dani suddenly shifted forward in her seat. 'Unless, Peggy Fisher didn't know that her husband was working cash-in-hand. *She* discovered the money that afternoon and confronted her husband about it.'

'That could have been the argument which triggered the homicides,' Annie agreed, sitting back down and cradling the steaming cup in her hands. 'If we can find out where Eric has stored that money, it could prove the man's guilt, once and for all.'

'Aye,' Dani replied steadily. 'I think it could.'

Chapter 15

It wasn't a particularly warm day, but Dani noticed that Sally Irving-Bryant had the sheen of sweat visible on her top lip. The lawyer was filling in forms at the front desk of HMP Edinburgh - known to its inmates simply as, 'Saughton Jail'.

Bevan had called her friend to request that she accompany Sally on her next visit to see Eric Fisher. The man agreed to have the detective present.

They were led by a prison guard to a large room with a small table in the centre of it. Within a few minutes, Eric was guided into the room to join them. A guard sternly directed him to sit straight down on one of the plastic chairs.

Fisher kept his head lowered during this process. Dani carefully took in the man's appearance. He was tall and muscular, with dark brown hair displaying only the odd fleck of grey. When he raised his eyes towards Sally, Bevan could see that Fisher was handsome, in a rugged, weather-beaten kind of way. The detective tried not to stare, but her eyes were drawn to the ugly, jagged scar on his neck, which was only partially covered by his shirt collar.

'Good morning Eric,' Sally began brusquely. 'How are you – are they still treating you well?'

The two women settled into the seats opposite.

The man shrugged his broad shoulders. 'I'm under protection, if that's what you mean. There aren't very many child killers in here. It makes me an attractive target. I get the feeling that the Governor doesn't want me standing in the dock covered in bruises.'

Sally flicked her blond hair, ignoring this comment. 'Eric. I'd like to introduce you to DCI Danielle Bevan, from the Police Scotland Serious Crime Division. She's been investigating the information you gave me. I invited her here so that she could feed back her conclusions.'

Fisher turned his head in Dani's direction. He let his eyes slide slowly down from her face to her breasts, where his vision lingered for a while. Bevan wondered if this was an attempt to be intimidating, or was simply how he greeted women.

'I'm pleased to meet you,' she said coolly.

Fisher nodded, but his expression remained impassive.

'I want to run through a few more of the details in your testimony.' Sally brought a sheaf of papers out of her file and spent ten minutes discussing the minutiae of his statement. Finally, the lawyer broached the subject of their defence. 'DCI Bevan found out some more information about your case this week.' The woman paused and looked towards her companion.

Dani understood this as a prompt to take over. 'Mr Fisher, I need to clear up a couple of important matters with you.'

Eric directed his steely gaze at the police officer. 'Did you find evidence of the man who was in my house?'

'I'm afraid there are still no forensic pointers to indicate a third party was in your property on the day that Peggy and the children were killed.'

Fisher slammed his fist on the table. Sally jumped nearly a foot in the air. The guard by the door took a step forward, but Dani waved him back.

'There must be! That bastard can't have broken into my house, butchered my family and sauntered out again without leaving a single trace.'

'Between the time that you were assaulted in the kitchen and when your neighbour arrived at the scene, there would have been an opportunity for this intruder to wipe away his prints. However, the fact remains that splatters of Callum and Peggy's blood were found on *your* clothing. This will be a major plank in the prosecution case.' Dani leaned in closer, trying to analyse his reaction.

'I *told* the police, when they questioned me at the hospital, that the guy who dragged me downstairs must have transferred the blood onto me from his clothes.'

'But the traces were the result of blood *splatters* – of the type which would be released at the time that the knife entered the body. A transferral mark would have been more like a smear – from one piece of material to another, for example.'

'Are you just here to re-hash the police case for me?' He shot an angry look at Sally. 'I thought you were on my side?'

'She is,' Dani replied sternly. 'We have to examine the evidence against you as thoroughly as the prosecution team will. Only then can the allegations be properly denied or refuted. There *is* a flaw in their forensic evidence. From what I can tell, their expert witness doesn't believe there was enough blood residue on your clothing to be consistent with you being the sole attacker.'

'That's correct,' Sally chipped in. 'I intend to put that argument forward very strongly in my cross-examination.'

Eric shook his head irritably. 'But it still suggests I was involved in killing Peggy and Callum.'

Dani took a deep breath. 'We found out that you were working on the River View Estate in the months leading up to the deaths of your wife and children.

Why didn't you inform the police about this?'

Fisher flashed Bevan a look which made her blood run cold. 'Who told you that?'

'There are plenty of witnesses who saw you carrying out the work. I'm amazed the information didn't come out at the time. You were receiving your pay cash-in-hand, according to the construction company. What happened to that money, Eric? If the cash was in the house then it's a motive for the break-in you have alleged.'

The man shifted about in his seat. 'The money wasn't in the house. I paid Craig what was due to him. The rest went on boozing at the pub and other stuff. Callum had just had his 12th birthday. I'd treated him to a few games for his Xbox. There was no money left, DCI Bevan.' For the first time, Eric Fisher met her gaze properly and adopted an open expression. Tears had sprung to his eyes at the mention of Callum's birthday.

'Did your wife know about this job you were doing? Obviously, you hadn't declared the earnings to the Revenue.'

Fisher sighed heavily. '*Of course* Peggy knew about it. Craig and I used to stop round ours for a cup of tea after we'd finished for the day. Peggy helped me to choose the fittings for the kitchens. I always felt bad because I couldn't provide the same for us.' He sat back in his seat, looking defeated.

'What about Craig O'Connor – could he have been the man who attacked you and placed the hood over your head?'

Eric snorted. 'Craig? He's a lanky streak of piss. I'd have shaken him off in an instant and so would Callum.' His face became deadly serious. 'The man who dragged me down those stairs was big and he was strong. That much I know for certain.'

'And you'll be sticking to that story in court,

then?' Sally said with undisguised exasperation.

Fisher jerked his head back towards the lawyer. 'It's not a *story*, sweetheart. It's the sodding truth.'

*

Bevan gave Sally a lift back to the townhouse she shared with her husband in the centre of Edinburgh. Dani's friend kept moving about in her seat as if she couldn't get comfortable, flipping down the sun visor and touching up her make-up in the mirror.

'Well, there's absolutely nothing more I can do for him now. I'll put his side of the argument as best I can in court. If the jury don't buy his flimsy version of the events, Eric Fisher will be in prison for the rest of his life.'

'I don't believe that Fisher can have spent all the money he made from working on the River View Estate. We're talking about several thousands of pounds.' Dani squinted against the fierce glare of the lowering sun.

Sally started counting points off on her fingers, 'beer, expensive computer games, the bookies, to name just a few potential recipients of Fisher's undeclared earnings. Not to mention their monthly subscription to Sky TV.'

'Did you ever consider the possibility that Fisher *paid* someone to attack his family?' Dani shot her companion an enquiring glance.

'What? Someone who half killed Fisher in the process and then rigged the set-up so it looked like *he* was to blame for the entire blood-bath? It doesn't make any sense, Dani.'

'Perhaps the arrangement went wrong. Fisher didn't pay the guy enough, or backed out of their agreement at the last moment – something that made this man pissed off enough to take revenge on the whole family.'

'Or maybe, it's exactly as it appears, and Eric Fisher *is* actually to blame for the entire blood-bath.'

Dani pulled onto the driveway next to a brand new Mercedes. Sally twisted round to lift her briefcase from the back seat, pausing to address her friend. 'Thanks for your help with this. I appreciate it. Most high ranking detectives would have told me where to get off.'

Dani smiled. 'I've not completely given up yet. There are a few more avenues I'd still like to try. If I uncover anything else, I'll let you know.'

Sally was already out of the car. She gave Bevan a wave, striding purposefully towards the grand front door, leaving the DCI suspecting that even if *she* hadn't entirely given up on this case, Fisher's lawyer most certainly had.

Chapter 16

'But what did you make of *him*?' Andy Calder interrupted, as Dani described her trip to Saughton. The Detective Constable was reclining comfortably on the sofa in Bevan's office, where she was catching up on the paperwork that had built up whilst she was away.

'I thought he was telling the truth,' Dani said casually, 'which, of course, means absolutely nothing.'

Andy adopted a puzzled expression. 'How come?'

'Well, the man very likely believes every word he is saying. That doesn't mean it's what actually happened. The guy totally flips out and murders his entire family – right? You don't have to be a psychologist to know that Fisher is going to have to construct a pretty good defence mechanism in his own head in order to deal with the reality of that.'

Calder nodded. 'So, his subconscious mind comes up with this intruder theory.'

'A theory that the evidence simply doesn't back up, which means we need to assume that it's false.'

'Okay, that's the most logical conclusion. But what do you think – after meeting the guy?'

Dani sighed. 'I can't get this Dundee murder out of my head. My instincts tell me it's linked to the Fisher killings.'

'Then make sure that DI Alexander keeps you in the loop. If something crops up in his investigation that might connect it to the Dalkeith case, you can follow it up. Other than that, there's not much else you can do.'

Bevan knew this was good advice. She paused for a moment before asking, 'I hope Carol wasn't too upset with us the other day?'

Dani noticed Andy's cheeks redden. She'd never seen him blush before. He wasn't the type.

'It was nothing. Carol doesn't usually bother about that kind of thing. She's just got a lot on her mind at the moment.' Andy shifted his weight forward, making to get up. Then he stopped and cleared his throat. 'We've been trying for another baby.'

Dani beamed. 'That's great news. How old is Amy now – coming up for two? It's the perfect age gap.'

Calder kept his gaze fixed on a piece of carpet somewhere near Dani's feet. 'I took a bit of persuading at first. With the heart attack and everything, I didn't want to tempt fate. Carol was heavily pregnant when I nearly died. She and Amy could have been left all alone. I suppose I felt frightened by the idea of going through all that again.'

'I can understand your fears. But there's absolutely no reason to think that way. You're so much fitter now than you were back then.'

'I know, and I gradually came around to the idea. But now it's taking longer than we thought it would. Carol's becoming upset about it. She thinks something might be wrong with one of us.'

Andy had never confided anything so personal to Dani before. She decided that he mustn't have anyone else he could talk to about it. 'Have you gone for tests? It might be that the drugs you're taking aren't helping the process.'

Calder finally looked up. 'That may be so, but they're helping *me* to stay alive. I don't want to come off my medication in order to give Carol another baby. I know it's selfish. You hear of women who are told that to carry a baby full-term would probably kill them, but they do it anyway. It's not like that for me. I'm happy with just the three of us.'

Bevan was momentarily speechless. 'I'm sure Carol must feel like that too. She'd never suggest taking an action which might damage your health. Once she's properly considered the risks, I'm sure she'll see it your way. You've got to *talk* to her about it, Andy.'

His handsome face looked pained. 'I'll try, Ma'am. But it's like she's become fixated on having another child. I don't think it'll matter what I say.' The man got slowly to his feet, walking solemnly out through the door, pulling it gently shut behind him.

*

'Poor Andy,' Huw Bevan commented evenly. 'When a woman is gripped by the desire to have a baby, it can be all consuming.'

Dani walked over to the patio doors which led out to her tiny garden, holding the phone to her ear. This was the kind of topic she usually tried to avoid discussing with her father. 'Did Mum ever want to have more children?'

'Oh aye, but Moira was so ill after you were born that it was really out of the question. She loved having a baby. That was never the issue. It just seemed that her chemical make-up wasn't suited to being pregnant.'

Dani decided not to say any more on the subject. She knew that these days, with the proper medication and guidance, women who suffered from postnatal depression were able to go on to have more children. There was no point in raising this issue with her dad. He would only think she was blaming him for not doing more to help her mum back then. 'How is the building work over near Jilly's place coming along?'

'They've started churning up the ground now. Goodness only knows how deep those foundations need to go. Jilly is convinced it will take generations for the wildlife to think it's safe to return. I wonder if the disruption is really worth it, for four weeks of use throughout the year.'

Dani suddenly had a thought. 'Do you know which building company are carrying out the work?'

'It's emblazoned across all of their vans and equipment, but I forget the name now. Hold on, I'll just take a look with my binoculars.' Huw came back onto the line after a couple of minutes. 'Bryant Construction.'

'Hmm, that's interesting,' Dani responded quietly and her father spent the rest of the call talking about how his garden was displaying all the signs that spring was finally on its way.

Chapter 17

Louise Keene was busy laying dust sheets across the furniture in the living room. She'd asked her neighbour to take the boys to school, so she would be at home when the builders arrived.

It was her husband's idea to have the extension built. Their semi-detached house was in the heart of an estate a mile outside of Glenrothes town centre. Although very well appointed, it was a little small.

The property was brand new when they bought it. Now the boys were getting older, the family had become desperate for more living space. Fergus had been putting in crazy hours at his insurance firm to secure a pay rise, which had finally been agreed the previous month. This meant that work could start on the ground floor extension they'd been planning.

Louise's parents, Joy and Bill, had offered to chip in some money to help pay for it, but Fergus was a proud man and didn't want to go cap-in-hand to his in-laws. Louise would happily have taken the money, so that she wasn't left looking after Jamie and Ben all on her own. Louise loved her boys to bits, but they were one hell of a handful. She was sure her mum and dad had been thinking along the same lines. They'd offered the money in order to help their daughter out. Her husband hadn't seemed to appreciate that fact.

A white van pulled up at the kerb, with the logo of the local firm they were using printed across the side. Louise opened the front door and let in the two men. One was in his fifties and the other significantly younger – late thirties she thought. The older man introduced them as Col and Davy.

Louise immediately put the kettle on, reaching for the tea bags and packet of sugar she'd bought in especially. Whilst the water was boiling, Louise rested her hands on the draining board and watched the men carrying their equipment through the side passage and out into the garden. She decided that Davy was quite attractive. He was tall and muscly with a mop of light brown, wavy hair. Louise had noticed him looking at her when they arrived, as if he were assessing her prettiness. She'd got the sense then that he liked what he saw.

Louise shook her sleek, dark bob and smiled, turning back to prepare the drinks. She was happily married and such thoughts were ridiculous. But Louise had missed having Fergus around these last few months, although the woman would never have admitted that she'd been lonely.

Lifting a tray onto the worktop, she added the mugs of tea. Pausing for a moment, Louise decided to open a packet of biscuits, which she fanned out on a plate. Using her bottom to push open the kitchen door, the young mum strode cheerfully out into the bright morning sunlight.

*

Bevan received a phone call at her desk, just before she was about to rip open the plastic wrapping on a pre-packed sandwich. It was from DI Alexander.

'I hope I'm not stopping you from going out to lunch?' He asked kindly, sounding genuinely sorry to disturb her.

'Not at all. Has there been a development?'

'I've been liaising with the profiler that your department recommended – Dr McAllister. She's been extremely helpful. With her advice, we've come up with a possible suspect. I wondered if you'd like to sit in on the interview.'

Dani shuffled forward. 'I'd like that very much, yes. When are you bringing him in?'

There was an awkward pause. 'One of my DCs is currently making the arrest. I hope to speak with the man sometime this afternoon.'

'I'd better get a move on then,' she added dryly.

*

The Detective Inspector had agreed to delay the interview until Dani arrived. Gordon Alexander appeared in a much better mood than when they'd last met. He held out one of his large hands as she stepped through a heavy door which led into the bowels of the police station. Dani shook it vigorously, imagining the man being quite at home on the rugby pitch, tightly gripping the patchwork leather of the oval ball.

'He's in Interview Room 1,' Alexander began. 'I'm letting him stew for a while.'

'What can you tell me about the man? I've not had chance to read the notes you e-mailed me yet.'

'Dr McAllister suggested that the perpetrator would be male, aged between 25 and 40, and would most likely have a manual job requiring few academic qualifications. With the individual knowing the layout of the property and potentially being aware of Morna's comings and goings, McAllister thought he might have been employed to carry out some work on the premises in the recent past.' Gordon continued to stride along the narrow corridor, talking as they walked.

'It sounds like a profile of Eric Fisher,' she muttered to herself, before saying more loudly, 'so whose name came up?'

'Tommy Galt, aged 29. He was born in Perth but now lives in Dundee with his girlfriend. Tommy is an electrician. According to Lyle Murphy, the man re-wired the property about six months ago. When my DC questioned the guy yesterday, he admitted to having sexual intercourse with Morna Murphy on several occasions.'

'Shit. Have *you* spoken with him yet?'

Gordon shook his head. 'This is the first contact I've had with the suspect.'

They'd reached the door of the interview room. DI Alexander gave a perfunctory knock and led the way inside.

Tommy Galt was seated at the table with his head resting in his hands. A duty solicitor occupied the chair next to him.

Alexander took his time, placing down a large file and clearly stating the names of those present for the tape. 'Mr Galt,' he said finally. 'I am questioning you in connection with a very serious crime. Do you know what that crime is?'

The young man lifted his head, his sandy blond hair standing up in tufts where he'd been running his hands through it. 'It's about the murder of Mrs Murphy.'

'That's correct. Could you tell us how you came to meet Morna Murphy?'

'They'd had some trouble with their electrics. The trip switch kept going off when Mr Murphy turned on his new TV. He called me up one Sunday evening. I said I could come round and take a look the next day, at 9am.'

'Was Lyle Murphy present when you arrived at the house on that Monday morning?'

Tommy shook his head, looking forlorn. 'No, it was just Morna. She showed me where the fuse box was and left me to it. It didn't take long to work out that the wiring was a mess. I said I could make it safe for now, but really, the whole place needed doing.'

'What did Mrs Murphy say to that?'

'She said she'd have to ask her husband.'

'And he instructed you to re-wire the property?'

'Yes, he called me that evening. I said I'd start in a few days from then, after I'd picked up all the stuff I'd need for the job.'

'What was your first encounter with Mrs Murphy like?' Dani enquired. 'Was she friendly towards you?'

Tommy's cheeks flushed. 'She was flirty.'

'Did you respond?'

'Yeah, I did. Morna was very attractive. But nothing happened during that first week. I've got a serious girlfriend. We're getting married next year. I had a mate helping me out and we got our heads down and did the job.'

'I'll need the name of your *mate*,' Alexander cut-in.

'Sure, he was only there with me for a couple of days. When the job was finished, Mrs Murphy wasn't in the house, so I had to pop back later on, in the early evening.'

'So, there were times when you were left alone in the property?'

He nodded. 'Sometimes, yes. When I came back, she'd just got out of the shower and was wearing a towelling dressing gown. Morna was taking her time finding the cheque book. She said that Lyle would be out that evening and offered me a drink.' He shrugged his muscular shoulders. 'Things just developed from there.'

'Where did you have sex with Mrs Murphy?' Alexander looked at the man levelly.

Tommy cleared his throat. 'In the bedroom.'

Bevan and Alexander exchanged glances.

'How long did this sexual relationship continue?'

'For a couple of months. Then we both got bored with it. That's the God's honest truth.' His eyes darted from one officer to the other. 'The sex was only a bit of fun. Morna initiated it. When she said the fling was over, I was perfectly happy about it. I'd been starting to worry that Lisa might find out. The last time I saw or heard anything about Morna was around Christmas last year - before she was killed and it was all over the news that is.'

'Have you been on the Murphys' estate in recent weeks, Tommy? We've got a photograph of your van. We'll be showing it to the neighbours.'

'I wired up an extension for a friend of mine on Falcon Road. That was at the end of January. Some of the residents might have seen my van parked up then. But I swear I've not been back since.'

'Do you give permission for a swab of your DNA to be taken for forensic comparison?'

Tommy Galt looked wary. 'I was in and out of that house for months. I had sex with Morna in their bed. How are you going to know if my DNA is present there simply because of what we did together all those months ago?'

Alexander laid his hands on the table so that the palms faced upwards. 'Our technicians have a way of working that kind of thing out,' he explained reasonably.

'Okay,' Tommy replied, although he still looked nervous. 'I'll give you a sample.'

The DI sat back and smiled.

But Dani felt uncomfortable too. She wasn't actually sure if the techies could do anything of the sort.

Chapter 18

Gordon Alexander led Dani up a flight of stairs to his desk in the corner of an open-plan office floor. It was neat and tidy and nicely positioned to take advantage of the view of the Tay Bridge visible through the large windows.

Alexander pulled out a chair for her, in a gesture which Dani thought was touchingly old-fashioned.

'Would you like a coffee?' He asked with concern. 'You've had a long drive today.'

'I'm fine, thank you.' Dani waited until the man was seated before enquiring, 'will you be looking to charge Galt?'

'One of my DCs is taking the DNA swab now. We've already got his fingerprints. It will all depend on what we can get back on those from the lab.' Alexander glanced at his watch. 'I can only keep him for another six hours. Most likely they'll be no charges brought just yet.'

'Why do you think Galt admitted so quickly to having a sexual relationship with Morna?'

'I believe that Tommy must know we'll find his DNA all over that house. If he admits to having had sex with Morna in there – especially in the bedroom – then Galt can claim it was from the time he was having a relationship with her.'

Dani nodded. 'It's definitely a possibility. Were the details of Morna's death reported in the press?'

The DI shook his head. 'No, we kept all information to a minimum. If this guy is innocent, he won't be aware that Morna was murdered in the bedroom.'

'Has he got any previous convictions?'

'A few, but they're related to driving violations, nothing involving violence against women or house-breaking.'

'What did Morna Murphy's *post mortem* throw up? Was there any evidence of recent sexual activity?'

'No, Morna hadn't had sex in the twelve hours before her murder. Lyle told us they'd not slept together for several days before she was killed.'

'Which doesn't mean she wasn't sleeping with somebody else,' Dani added. 'If Morna really did split up with Tommy Galt last Christmas, there could have been another man on the scene by now. If there was no sexual violence, what do you think Galt's motive would have been – was the intention always to rob the Murphys' place?'

Alexander shrugged his shoulders. 'Maybe he found out there *was* another boyfriend. Sexual jealousy perhaps?'

Dani frowned. 'But then I would expect a sexual assault of some description, as Galt tried to reassert his claim over her.'

'Wasn't the frenzied stabbing a kind of violation?'

Dani could see where the man was coming from, but the psychology didn't quite wash with her. 'If the knife was aimed at her breasts and genitals I might agree with you, but the wounds were predominantly to her back and shoulders. I'd run the theory past Dr McAllister, but in my opinion, this wasn't a sexually motivated crime.'

The DI smiled, seemingly content to defer to her greater experience in homicide cases. He glanced out of the window as the lights on the bridge flickered into life. The sky was rapidly darkening. Alexander's face creased with concern. 'Are you driving back to

Glasgow tonight?'

'I'm going to stay with some friends on the way. In fact, I'd better make tracks.' Dani pushed back her chair and stood up.

'Thank you so much for your input, DCI Bevan. I'm finding your advice extremely valuable.'

The detective smiled broadly. 'Not at all. Do let me know about the forensic results.' She paused for a moment, 'and please call me Dani.'

*

The Hutchisons' house in Falkirk was warm and welcoming. Joy was re-heating a plate of food for their guest. The aroma hit Dani as she came downstairs after freshening up. The DCI took a seat at the kitchen table.

'It smells great,' she said, suddenly ravenous.

'Oh, it's nothing much,' the lady replied.

Bill strode into the room, a broad smile on his face. 'That was Louise on the phone. She says the builders are making good progress.'

Dani looked puzzled.

'Our daughter and son-in-law are having an extension built onto their wee house in Glenrothes, Detective Inspector. You can't begin to imagine how difficult it's been to pin a contractor down to do the job. You'd think these people didn't want the work.' Bill accepted a glass of wine from his wife and sat opposite Dani whilst she ate.

'Does much building work go on in *your* estate?' The detective asked casually.

'The houses are larger here. Most have a generously sized fourth bedroom. It doesn't stop folk putting on a conservatory or adding an attic room, we've had a fair bit of that in recent years.'

Dani nodded, absorbing this piece of information.

Bill leant forward. 'Are you asking that because it has something to do with the case in Dundee? Do the police believe the murder was committed by a local tradesperson? I suppose it would make sense. These folk get to know the layout of properties very well.'

Bevan couldn't help but smile. There was no point in trying to sneak anything past Bill. 'The SIO is thinking along those lines, yes. Did Rita have any work done on her place recently?'

Bill considered this and then shook his head.

Joy padded back in from the utility room. 'She had her downstairs carpets cleaned, if that's the kind of thing you mean. The doctor recommended it, if you can believe that. Apparently, he thought that removing some of the dust mites would help her emphysema. I told Rita it was pure nonsense. The chemicals these machines pump out would be far worse for her, but of course, the doctor's word is always sacrosanct to folk of her age. Remember, Bill? We joked at the time that perhaps the surgery had shares in the cleaning company.'

'Oh yes, I do recall now. It was about a month ago.'

Dani took a final mouthful and pushed aside her empty plate. 'That was lovely, Joy, thanks.'

Bill put down his glass with a flourish. 'Of course! The company had that totally ridiculous slogan plastered across the side of the van – 'we pamper your piles' – I suppose it gets them noticed.'

Dani chuckled. 'They weren't making any attempt to be inconspicuous then.'

'Do you think those carpet men can have had something to do with Rita's burglary?'

Bevan shrugged her shoulders. 'It's a line of inquiry worth pursuing. The police could try to identify a pattern in the area. A certain tradesperson may have carried out work at all the houses that were broken into, for example. If I were the SIO, I'd put a couple of DCs on the task.'

Joy's expression suddenly darkened. 'Should we be concerned about Louise and the boys - in the house for all that time with the men building their extension?'

Dani put out her hand and rested it on the woman's arm. 'Not at all. I shouldn't really have mentioned anything about it. I'm certainly not suggesting that all building contractors are dangerous. Louise is using a reputable local firm, isn't she?'

'Oh yes,' Bill added with feeling. 'We insisted upon it.'

'Then there's absolutely nothing to worry about.'

Chapter 19

The sun was just emerging from behind the clouds as Huw Bevan proceeded towards the front door of his bungalow. He could see his neighbour, Jilly O'Keefe, standing on the other side of the glass.

'I'm sorry to bother you, Huw. But I'd like to beg your assistance for a moment,' she said matter-of-factly, after he'd opened up.

'Of course.' Huw lifted his padded jacket off the hook and slipped his feet into a pair of wellington boots.

The retired headmaster allowed his friend to lead the way along the narrow path at the top of the beach, until they reached the stone wall which marked out the boundary of Jilly's windswept garden.

But Jilly bypassed her own property, taking Huw instead towards the wee bothy which lay another quarter of a mile up the hill. As they grew closer, Huw could see the extent of the earthworks that were being constructed in order to make the cottage larger. For the moment, the machinery was at a standstill and there were no workmen in sight.

'Come and look at this,' the woman entreated.

Jilly was heading purposefully towards a small mound, on top of which was one of Colonsay's historical cairns; a monument constructed out of stones, which was said to have been there since one of the clan battles of the seventeenth century. According to legend, the army of ordinary clansfolk would each place a stone on the cairn at the start of the battle. The ones who survived would return to the cairn and remove their stone, leaving the rest as a memorial to the men who'd been killed.

Huw Bevan could see that a large proportion of this particular cairn had already started to subside, as the foundations being built for the bothy extension had undermined the hill upon which it had stood for many hundreds of years.

'I told the workmen they'd have to stop,' Jilly pronounced. 'I pointed out that they were damaging an important historical monument. The foreman looked at me as if I'd just come down in a spacecraft. To them, it's clearly just a pile of stones.'

Huw shook his head solemnly and tutted. 'We'll need to call a meeting at the Town Hall. I'd like to ask Kenny McKinley how the plans for this work ever got approved.'

Jilly adopted an aggressive stance, with her sturdy legs in brightly patterned woollen tights positioned wide apart, as if she were about to challenge someone to fisty-cuffs. 'Obviously, the planners have received some kind of *incentive*. I objected to the plans. The new building will be far too close to my place. Of course, the council took no notice.'

'That's a serious allegation, Jilly. We need to approach this issue calmly and through the correct channels. Who owns the land, do you know?'

'Ronald Cross sold the bothy to that English chap, the academic. He came here on holiday for a good few years – do you remember? Then he got Parkinson's disease and couldn't travel this far north. I believe he finally died last year. The family quickly passed on the bothy to developers. It's some faceless organisation that we're dealing with now. Bryant's Construction, it's called.'

Huw nodded, thinking about the visit that he and Dani had received from the well-dressed lawyer woman. He immediately wondered if this construction company was as faceless as Jilly feared.

*

Louise felt as if she'd done nothing except make endless cups of tea for the past week. Dust seemed to lie thickly on every surface in the house. As soon as she cleared it up, another layer soon settled in its place. But worse than this, Ben's asthma was playing up, what with all the particles floating about in the atmosphere. He'd been told to stay home from school, although his mother knew this wasn't the best place for him to be. She'd set the lad up in her and Fergus' room, which was situated at the front of the property. He had the portable TV set in there and the window wide open, to let in some fresh air.

She lowered herself onto a kitchen chair with a heavy sigh, as Davy Burns strutted in with his empty mug.

'Is everything okay, Mrs Keene?' He immediately asked, observing her hunched posture.

To her great embarrassment, Louise began to cry. The tears leaked down her cheeks in what felt like an unsightly torrent. The man carefully placed his cup on the draining board, pulled out a seat and sat down, just inches away from her. 'Come on, love, what's the matter?'

Davy's tone was so kind and gentle, Louise thought the sobs would never subside, but eventually, they did. 'I'm just so tired. My husband is always at work and the boys never stop, you know?'

He nodded. 'My brothers and I were like that when we were little. We gave my poor mum one hell of a run around. But before long, she was having a battle to get us out of bed. It doesn't last forever.'

Louise looked up, examining his clear green eyes.

'I know this extension will make things easier in the end, but it's bloody hard whilst it's going on.' She managed a weak smile.

Davy rummaged in his pocket for a handkerchief, which he proceeded to use to gently dab at the watery streaks on her cheeks. With his other hand, he cradled her head, running Louise's soft, silky hair through his fingers. She closed her eyes, allowing him to place his lips over hers. The reassuring sensation that the warmth of his touch gave her made Louise want to cry again, but she didn't. The woman slipped her arm around his broad back instead and pulled him closer. 'My eldest is just upstairs,' she murmured.

'It's okay,' he whispered. 'I only want to hold you for a while, until you're feeling better.'

Louise rested her head on his shoulder, finally relaxing into his arms and allowing all of her anxieties to drift away.

She truly wished they could remain like this forever.

Chapter 20

DCI Bevan placed down the receiver of her telephone with a clatter before re-joining Andy Calder in the kitchen of her flat. Somehow, they'd got used to working on the Fisher case from there. The process didn't feel quite the same when they were at the Pitt Street Headquarters.

'Nothing's wrong, is it Ma'am?' Andy enquired with genuine concern, noting her furrowed brow.

Dani sighed. 'Not really, I've just received a lecture on the clan battles of Colonsay from my father. He wants me to help him and the islanders go to war against Bryant Construction. To be honest, I could do without the distraction right now.'

'Ah, the legendary clan Macfie and their rivalry with the Macdonalds.' Andy lifted his mug of tea with a big grin on his face.

'Next time Dad calls, I'll pass the phone over to you. Seriously, what do you know about the Macfies?'

'It was the only thing I was ever interested in at school,' Andy explained. 'The Macfies held the balance of power in Colonsay for hundreds of years, right up until the early 17th Century, when the last chief of the clan was executed and the island fell into the hands of the Macdonalds. I had an illustrated book about it when I was a kid. I must dig it out for Amy.'

'Apparently, Bryant Construction's new building conversion threatens to destroy one of the ancient cairns on the island. The monument is positioned on a Macfie battle site. Dad wants me to have a word with Sally Irving-Bryant about it.'

Andy puffed out his cheeks, looking aggrieved. 'I'm not surprised the islanders are upset. This company can't go around blithely destroying the heritage of Scotland in that way.'

Dani decided she'd finally stumbled upon a cultural issue that Andy was passionate about. The DCI could see how the history of the highland clans might appeal to Calder, with its emphasis on the ordinary men of Scotland fighting to preserve their way of life against invaders, usually from the English ruling classes.

But it wasn't the kind of crusade she was inclined to pursue at this particular time. Bevan swiftly tried to steer the conversation back to the case. 'I spoke with DI Tait at eastern. He sent a pair of detectives out to question the Fishers' near neighbours, to see if they'd had any building work done in the last couple of years. He's given me the details of two local firms.'

'Was any work carried out at the Fisher property itself?'

'It doesn't sound like it. I expect that if anything needed doing, Eric would take on the job himself.'

Andy frowned. 'Then I don't see the connection, Ma'am. These builders would have to be *inside* the Fishers' place to be able to case the joint for a break-in.'

Dani ran her fingers through her hair, thinking she had to agree. The suspect that DI Alexander had in custody made the Dundee murder appear quite different in character from what happened to Peggy Fisher and her children.

'The only possible connection,' Andy continued, 'was if Peggy had a lover like Morna Murphy did. That's where I could see all that anger and aggression stemming from. It would also explain why the murderer might want to frame Eric Fisher.'

Bevan nodded, glancing at the wedding photograph on the table in front of her. 'The case just seems to keep coming back to Peggy Fisher.' She tapped her finger on the grainy image. 'I don't believe we've understood the woman properly yet.'

'Then that should be where we start looking next.' Andy set down his empty mug with a heavy and decisive thud, gathering up the notes and slipping them back into the file, as if the DC really meant business.

*

'Are you interested in booking a spring break?' Asked the attractive woman who was seated behind one of the desks. She wore a blue uniform and a full face of make-up. Her appearance reminded Dani of a stewardess on one of the more upmarket airlines.

The DCI held up her warrant card. 'We aren't customers, I'm afraid.'

The woman sighed, gesturing for them to take a seat. 'Is this about Peggy? I thought there'd be more questions before the trial started. As if her poor family haven't suffered enough.'

'Did you know Peggy Fisher well?' Andy enquired gently.

The woman tipped her head towards the empty workstation to her right. 'She sat there beside me pretty much every working day for two years so I'd say so, yes.' She shook her bleach-blond locks. 'Sorry, it's just very hard not to feel bitter when such a lovely young mum gets struck down in her prime. I'm Annette, by the way.'

'Did you ever see Mrs Fisher outside of work?'

'Occasionally. But I've not got children and Peggy

had three, including the wee twins, who were really hard work, God bless them. She came out for drinks with me and my mates maybe once a month.'

'Did she talk to you, confide in you?' Dani leant in closer, looking intently at the woman's artificially tanned face.

'About her marriage, do you mean? The American woman working with you lot already asked me dozens of questions about Eric, which was weird, because I'd hardly ever met the guy.'

'It's Peggy we're interested in,' Dani explained.

'Good. Somebody bloody-well should be.' Annette retrieved a hankie from her pocket and dabbed at non-existent tears. 'Peggy was beautiful and kind. She loved her children more than anything in the world. When I was having trouble with blokes, she always gave me the best of advice.'

'Was she happy?' Dani ventured.

Annette looked surprised by the question. 'Erm, I think so. She talked about Callum a lot, and the girls. They were very close as a family.'

'When she gave you advice on your relationships, did Peggy use her own marriage as an example – saying what kinds of things worked for her and Eric, I mean?'

The woman seemed genuinely stymied by this question. 'No, it was general stuff, about me needing to value myself and not put up with any shit.'

'Okay. What about her job here at the travel agency? Was Peggy popular with the clients, or had there been any disputes?'

Annette puffed herself up, obviously more comfortable with this topic. 'Oh, people just *loved* Peggy. She could get folk signed up for a Caribbean cruise when all they'd come in for was a week in Torremolinos.'

'Did any of the customers take a particular shine

to her? Was anyone hanging around the shop a bit too much in the months leading up to her death?'

The woman shook her head. 'Nobody suspicious.'

Dani stood up. 'Well, thank you very much for your time.'

As the detectives walked towards the door, Annette called after them. 'When I say nobody suspicious, I mean not some weirdo that she didn't already know. But in the weeks before Peggy was killed, her cousin was in a lot. It was something to do with discussing their grandmother's will.'

Andy lifted out his notebook. 'If you could give us her name, we'll check it out.'

Annette looked confused. 'Oh, it wasn't a woman. Her cousin is a man, he's called Mark.' She blushed. 'I kept badgering Peggy to bring him out to the pub with us one night. He was really dishy.'

Dani turned sharply on her heels. 'Would it be possible for you to provide us with a description of Peggy's cousin?'

She nodded. 'I suppose so. You know, I always thought it was strange, because I could never make out any family resemblance between them at all.'

Chapter 21

'I know her type,' Andy asserted confidently, flicking through his notebook as Dani drove them to the City and Borders Police Headquarters. 'Carol's got a couple of friends like her. They're totally obsessed with their own disastrous love lives and never listen to a word anyone else tells them.'

'I certainly don't believe that Peggy would have confided in Annette Walker. But the woman has provided us with a very detailed description of this 'Mark' chap.'

'It will be interesting to find out if Peggy actually *does* have a cousin of that name. How did Carmichael's team miss this piece of information?'

'The officers in charge had tunnel vision. Their investigation was entirely focussed on Eric Fisher. Not one of those witnesses was questioned closely about Peggy. It's as if she were considered completely irrelevant to the inquiry.'

*

Annie Carmichael looked uncomfortable. She'd called an impromptu briefing for the team who worked on the Fisher case. Bevan could see DI Mike Tait, his considerable bulk perched on a desk at the back.

'I've checked with the Wheelans. Peggy has no male cousins, let alone one called Mark. Both her grandmothers died over twenty years ago.' The DCI pointed to a list on a flip chart behind her. 'These are the key features of Annette's description. I've sent a DC out to speak with Ms Walker again to get an E-fit created.' She took a deep breath. 'This man needs to be found - as soon as bloody possible.'

Tait raised his hand and said, 'with respect, Ma'am, it's over a year since the murders. We could have asked around Dalkeith town centre at the time – in the cafés and pubs – to find witnesses who saw the pair of them together. But *now*, there isn't a hope in hell.'

His words hung heavy in the air. There wasn't much anyone could say to dispute his logic.

Dani stood up and moved to the front. 'I know this evidence is coming late to the party, but I've known cases to be re-opened after ten years when a new lead turns up. Peggy Fisher was a mum with two very young children. She can't have met this man far from home. He must be local. Even if he has now fled the area, *somebody* around here will know him.' The DCI stepped forward and caught the eye of each dejected looking detective. 'The existence of this man could mean one of two things; either *he* was the intruder that Eric claims was in the house when his family were killed, or his relationship with Peggy was discovered by Fisher and *that* was the trigger for the murders. For what it's worth, I still think that Eric Fisher did this. But you'll need to work this lead extremely hard if you want to prove it in court next week.'

Dani's speech received a few conciliatory nods and grunts. The officers began to disperse, heading back to their own desks with an air of determination.

Andy and Dani followed Annie Carmichael to her office. 'Thanks for that,' she muttered. 'It required someone from outside the investigation to give them the rocket they needed.'

Dani took a seat but Andy remained standing,

shifting his weight from one foot to the other irritably. 'There's one thing I can't get my head around. If this guy Mark isn't the person who killed Fisher's wife and kids, then why hasn't he come forward? You'd have thought he'd be banging down the door of the nearest cop shop to tell them he was Peggy's lover and that's why her husband did her in.'

'Unless he's married himself,' Annie answered slowly. 'That would explain why we've not heard a dicky bird from him.'

'Even so,' Andy pressed. 'It must have been difficult for him to keep quiet, if he had any feelings for Peggy at all.'

Bevan thought about this. She could appreciate the logic of both officers. If this 'Mark' character wanted to hold onto the life he still had, Dani could understand him disappearing off into the shadows. Some people could be extremely good at cutting their losses, mercenary as it may seem.

During this brief moment of silence, a dark-suited man appeared at the other side of the DCI's door. He gave it a tentative knock.

'Come in, DC Webber!' Carmichael boomed.

Dani placed the detective in his mid-thirties at most.

'I'm sorry to intrude, Ma'am.' He swivelled round to address Bevan. 'DI Tait told me that you'd requested information about local tradespeople who'd worked on the Fishers' estate.'

'That's right,' she replied, feeling a prickle of anticipation run up the back of her neck. 'Have you got something for us?'

'I'm not sure. It's just that when Mike mentioned a possible link to these house-breakings on the east coast it put me in mind of an old case I investigated, eight years back.'

'Go on.' Even though it wasn't her office, Dani

gestured for him to take one of the chairs.

'Do you recall the case of Diane and Albert Beattie?'

Bevan nodded, it was hard to forget.

'Miss Beattie lived in an old vicarage, down in the borders, with her elderly father. Diane was working from home at the time. Two men broke into the house late one Saturday afternoon. Whilst one of them ransacked the house, the other forced Diane to go upstairs with him. He raped her at knifepoint in one of the bedrooms.'

'Bastard,' Calder hissed. 'Did you get them?'

'Aye,' Webber continued. 'The rapist got fourteen years, he's still inside. The other guy was out in five.'

Andy's cheeks flushed crimson. 'What kind of sentence is five sodding years?'

'The other burglar claimed that he had no idea his accomplice was going to rape Diane. The plan was to commit a burglary, nothing else. Tim Flannigan took part in a victim mediation programme. This helped to reduce his jail time.'

'Did Flannigan meet with Diane and her father as part of the mediation?' Dani knew about the practice of bringing the perpetrators of violent crime face-to-face with their victims but had no first-hand experience of it.

'Diane and Tim became friends. They wrote to each other after the sessions were over. Di now runs a charity raising awareness about safety in the home, especially for women. She invites Tim to come and speak at their meetings sometimes. I go down and help her out when I can too. Prevention is much more satisfying to achieve than mopping up the mess left behind by violent crime.'

Andy looked entirely perplexed by the whole concept.

But Bevan was very impressed with what she'd

seen of this young detective. 'Do you think it would be worth my while talking to Diane Beattie?'

Webber nodded vigorously, fishing a business card out of his jacket pocket. 'This is her number. Di's worked with dozens of these cases, but from the other side. I reckon she could give you some pretty useful insights.'

Bevan gratefully received it. 'Thank you, Detective Constable. I believe you may well be right.'

Chapter 22

Dani had spent the previous evening reading through the case files of the Beattie burglary in 2007. The man who raped Diane Beattie was a nasty piece of work, with violent convictions dating back to his adolescence spent in various children's homes. Tim Flannigan had simply fallen in with the wrong crowd and got mixed up with drug taking. He was supporting a hefty crack cocaine addiction at the time of the break-in at the vicarage.

Bevan turned off the main road and drove through a narrow lane which wound past an impressive church built out of Scottish red sandstone. She knew the old vicarage was situated along one of the tracks which ran beside the graveyard. But Diane Beattie didn't live there any longer. According to the address Dani had, Diane's cottage was on the main street.

The village of Tweedvale was very attractive, nestled as it was beneath the Cheviot Hills and on the banks of the River Tweed. Despite this, Bevan was still amazed that Diane had chosen to stay on there after her ordeal eight years earlier. Her father, Albert Beattie, had died only a year later.

There was a space on the kerbside directly in front of the quaint little stone cottage where the woman now lived. Dani climbed out of the car and approached the tiny front door. Diane answered after only one knock. She smiled broadly, her silver hair cut into a neat, feathered style. Bevan knew she was now 56 years of age and had been 48 at the time she was attacked.

Dani was led along a dark corridor to a pleasant

sunroom at the rear, which looked out onto a surprisingly large garden.

'Folk are usually amazed at the length of my garden. It's considerable bigger than the house,' Diane commented, pre-empting any enquiry. 'If you look closely, you'll see that the river runs past us at the back. Our terrace couldn't have been built any closer because of the flood plain, which is very much to the residents' benefit. The garden is the reason I bought the place.'

Dani nodded and put out her hand. 'DCI Danielle Bevan. Please call me Dani.'

'I shall,' Diane replied. She disappeared into the little kitchen, rattling around with cups and plates. When Diane re-entered, she was carrying a tray of teas and cakes.

'Thank you. It's been a rather long drive.'

The hostess settled herself into an armchair and poured milk into their cups. 'So, you've been sent by my young friend, Alec.'

Dani looked puzzled. 'Oh, DC Webber. Yes, he thought you might be able to assist me.'

'With the Fisher case, he said. I must admit that I never considered that tragedy to have any bearing upon the work of our charity. I have no expertise in issues of domestic violence.'

'May I speak confidentially?'

'Of course,' Diane replied.

'Eric Fisher is claiming that an intruder murdered his family. I've been working with the team in Dundee who are investigating the stabbing of Morna Murphy last week. We've identified some potential links between the two crimes.'

Diane raised her eyebrows. 'Well, I must say I'm amazed. The press coverage made it sound as if the father was undoubtedly guilty. I suppose one never ceases to be fooled by what one reads in the papers.'

'Quite so. What type of work does your charity carry out?' Dani reached forward and selected a pink macaroon, suddenly feeling famished.

'There are two arms of the organisation. One deals with victim support and the other with prevention. I supervise both. We have already been in contact with the police in Dundee, to offer our assistance to poor Mr Murphy. A counsellor will be paying him a visit next week.'

'I expect that you've become familiar with a number of different cases through the work of your charity.'

'I've come into contact with scores of people affected by stranger violence in their homes, often spanning the length and breadth of Scotland. Some over the border, too.' Diane sipped her tea thoughtfully. 'Although the incidences may appear totally random and entirely financially motivated, I have identified certain patterns over the years.'

Dani shuffled closer, intrigued by the lady's insights.

'In many of the cases I've come into contact with, the individuals who were targeted by burglars had recently been featured in the local press for example. The level of exposure ranged in significance from people who'd won a rosette at a cake show to someone who'd just been elected as the local Member of Parliament. In my own case, my father had not long retired from his job in the Tweedvale solicitors' office. There'd been a lengthy piece about him in the paper the previous week.'

'Do you think this was how the perpetrators decided upon their victims?'

Diane shook her head. 'I don't believe it was anything as organised or conscious as that. I have asked the men themselves on various occasions, including Tim Flannigan. They always claimed not to have known anything about this publicity. In Tim's case, he couldn't read before he was imprisoned for the break-in at my house. He couldn't possibly have read the article about Dad.'

'Then how do you explain the coincidence?'

'Oh, I believe they certainly came into contact with the articles somehow, but the effect was entirely subconscious. In some respect, at least one of the perpetrators must have been guided towards a particular victim because of what they'd seen. It triggered a reaction for them – of envy perhaps. The person they saw in the photograph or on the TV news had achieved a status that they themselves knew they never would. The burglary was an attempt to take it away from them.'

Dani hadn't heard a theory like this one before. 'It makes you have second thoughts about doing interviews in the press.'

Diane smiled kindly, her green eyes twinkling. 'You shouldn't let the thought give you sleepless nights. This wasn't the only factor at play. The homes most at risk are isolated, sometimes on the edge of fields or farmland. In our case, it was the graveyard.' The woman chuckled wryly. 'That's why I now live in the middle of a cramped terrace.'

Dani considered this for a moment. 'But in Morna Murphy's case, their house was in the centre of a tightly packed estate. Cars and people were passing by all the time.'

'It is unusual, I agree. But new patterns emerge all the time as lifestyles change. On these soulless new estates, perhaps nobody notices what goes on any longer. The need for isolation has become less important to burglars.'

'What sort of advice do you give to people to avoid being a victim of these crimes?'

Diane knitted her fingers together. 'There are

absolutely no guarantees of protection, of course. What my speakers emphasise is the importance of personal vigilance. If you allow a person into your home, you must be sure to keep them at arm's length. There is a temptation to believe them to be your friend simply because you are interacting with them in a domestic setting. It adds a personal dimension to a situation that is in reality no more intimate than buying a magazine over the counter at a newsagents.'

'In Morna Murphy's case, we believe her attacker may have originally come into contact with her whilst re-wiring the property.'

Diane threw her hands up in the air. 'A textbook example. We must tread very carefully with the stranger who invades our home territory. I always recommend having a friend or relative there whilst the tradesperson visits. This appears to tip the balance towards creating a more professional atmosphere.'

Dani decided she would use this piece of advice when she next did outreach work. 'If you don't mind me asking, how many of your insights were gained through your own experience?'

She sighed heavily. 'Too many, Dani, too many. Duncan Copeland, the man who assaulted me, had been delivering our coal to us for months before the break-in occurred. It was Tim who I'd never set eyes on before.'

'I hadn't realised your attacker was known to you. It wasn't mentioned in the file.'

'We had him in for a cup of tea once, when the weather was very bad. I suppose that to his twisted mind, we'd invited him into our lives. He felt he could have whatever he wanted from us, to violate all we held dear.'

'I sincerely hope you never blamed yourselves for

what happened,' Dani replied indignantly.

'No, we never did. But I wanted to warn others. What we believe to be an act of innocent human kindness can be turned against us.' Diane leant forward, regarding her guest with scrutiny. 'There are evil people out there, DCI Bevan, those who would never dream of seeking forgiveness or absolution for their wickedness. For this reason, we must always be on our guard. Even without realising it, we could be opening the door to a terrible evil, allowing it to walk straight into our lives. After that, there's very little we can do to stop it from destroying us.'

Chapter 23

James Irving's Marchmont flat was a Victorian conversion with tall, sash and case windows looking down onto the quiet street. The place wasn't large, but the living room had enough space for a small dining table. James had laid it for dinner.

The newly fitted kitchen was through an archway. This was where Dani's host was pouring them out a couple of drinks. The area was extremely bijou, there wasn't even a window.

'It's a lovely flat,' she commented politely.

'*Small*, is the word you're searching for,' he replied with a grin. 'I decided to get myself a little bolt-hole here in the city. My eventual plan is to buy a house further out. On the east coast, maybe.'

'That's a good idea. You can actually commute from there.'

'But it would be a bit pointless on my own,' he said quietly, leading his guest back to the lounge. 'So, how is your investigation going? It has obviously brought you back over to this area. Can you tell me any more?'

Dani sat on the sofa, accepting her glass of wine. 'Actually, I can. I went to see Diane Beattie today. She campaigns to raise awareness of safety in the home. One of our DCs is friends with her. He thought she'd have some interesting insights into this spate of burglaries we're experiencing.'

'Did she?'

Bevan nodded. 'Diane has worked on so many cases in the last eight years that she's been able to identify patterns in the behaviour of offenders. I think that the Serious Crime Division should be working more closely with her charity.'

James furrowed his brow. 'Hang on, wasn't she the lady who was attacked at the vicarage? Her father was beaten up too, wasn't he?'

'Yes, Diane has dedicated her life now to preventing similar crimes. She's a very interesting woman.'

'There was a programme about her on the radio, a few years back. Diane met with one of the men who broke into her house. They took part in this rehabilitation project where perpetrators of crime confront their victims. At the time, I thought the woman must be some kind of saint. I'd have been tempted to wring his neck.'

'The man she met wasn't the one who had raped her and beaten up her father. Tim Flannigan was an illiterate drug-addict who was desperate for money. He wasn't aware there'd be anyone at home when they broke in. What his accomplice did in that house haunted him, too. That's why he wanted to meet with Diane.'

'But the guy could surely have stopped it. That's what I would find hard to forgive, that he stood by and allowed it to happen.' James looked indignant.

Dani shrugged her shoulders. 'I've read the transcript of their interviews. Flannigan claims that Copeland sought out the knife from the kitchen as soon as they were inside. He says the man was like something possessed. Flannigan feared that if he tried to intervene, Copeland would butcher them all. He was paralysed by fear.'

James was silent for a moment. 'Actually, that makes sense. When I was held prisoner by Micky Ford that time, I could do nothing to defend myself. I'm a tall, athletic sort of bloke but he was a maniac. I knew that if I fought back, he'd kill me, right then and there.'

'By forgiving Tim Flannigan, Diane released herself from some of the bitterness and anger.' Dani took a sip of her wine. 'Despite Diane's progressive approach to rehabilitating criminals, she said something strange to me this afternoon. It reminded me of a phrase that Sally used when she first spoke about the Fisher case.'

James raised an eyebrow quizzically.

'Diane suggested that there was some kind of wickedness at work in those violent break-ins, that people were allowing evil to enter their homes.'

'I'm surprised that *Sally* would ever use such a biblical term about one of her briefs. She's usually so rational.'

'Sally sensed a terrible evil present in the Fisher case. It's why she asked for my help in the first place.'

'Well, the killing of that poor woman and her children is the worst kind of crime. I'd be surprised if my sister weren't deeply affected by it. I don't think you should read any more into it than that.' James stood up, leaning forward to rest his hand on Dani's shoulder. 'Come on,' he said gently. 'Let's sit up and eat.'

*

Dani spent the night in James' bed, whilst he took the sofa. The DCI got up at the same time as her host and was out of the flat nice and early. She headed straight for the police headquarters in Fettes. Bevan requested some desk space and a computer, finding herself sharing a workstation with DC Alec Webber.

'How was Di?' He asked amiably.

'Very well,' Dani replied. 'She's a remarkable lady.'

'I knew that from the very first moment I met her, at the house, after her father had called us. Diane wanted to provide a statement straight away. She was incredibly brave.' Webber lowered his voice. 'In those days, the force weren't so good at dealing with cases of sexual assault. We had no female officer on the scene.' His expression became sheepish. 'I was living with my mum and three older sisters back then. I like to hope I looked after Diane okay in those first few hours.'

'I'm sure you did,' Dani replied firmly. 'That's why she's friends with you now.'

Bevan turned her attention back to the computer screen. She was performing a Google search on Peggy Fisher, to see if the woman had received any publicity in the months leading up to her death. Most local papers had an online version these days, so there should have been a record of any articles that Peggy was featured in. Dani could find nothing.

Then she tried Eric. He'd had some adverts placed in local online directories for his business, but there was nothing else relating to him before his family were killed, although there was plenty afterwards. The salacious assertions of his guilt in the tabloid press were enough to fill fifty search pages. After reading some of the vile stuff that was written about him she made a mental note never to Google herself.

Dani sat back in her seat and sighed. The Fisher family were fairly anonymous before the majority of them were butchered in their own home, which catapulted them to front page news across the UK. There was Peggy's job at the travel agency, however. That could have placed her within some creep's radar.

Bevan had a thought. Sitting forward again, she tried another search. This time, there was a result.

Callum Fisher had been the captain of one of Dalkeith's under 15s football squads. A month before the family were killed, Callum's team won the league. The story was featured by a number of local news outlets.

In one of the pieces, there was a picture of Callum holding the trophy, with his dad and grandad - Eric Fisher and Rob Wheelan, on either side of the boy. It seemed that the Fishers' eldest son had scored the last minute goal which decided the match. All three were named in the text and Eric was quoted as saying how proud he was of his boy.

Bevan printed off this particular article. She knew that Diane Beattie's patterns were purely hypothetical and certainly didn't prove anything, but Dani still found it strange that it appeared to fit the Fisher case too. The DCI wasn't entirely sure what it meant, but her first course of action would be to call DI Alexander in Dundee and encourage him to try the same trick out on Morna and Lyle Murphy.

Chapter 24

DI Gordon Alexander appeared pleased to see her. They'd arranged to meet up in a park to the west of the city centre. Alexander led Dani up Balgay Hill to Mills Observatory, where the views were impressive. It was cold, but Bevan was glad of the exercise.

The pair strolled around the austere sandstone structure, with the detective inspector pointing out the huge dome which had white shutters designed to pull back and reveal the telescope.

'I used to come here with my family,' he commented affably. 'My daughter loved the planetarium.'

Dani didn't quite know what to say to this, so she remained quiet.

'The forensic results came back on Tommy Galt.'

'Oh yes?' She was more comfortable with this line of conversation.

'We couldn't get a positive match on the DNA, the only traces we found in the house were Lyle and Morna's, but we identified his fingerprints on the door frame of the bedroom.'

'Is it possible they were left there when Galt and Morna were still in a relationship?'

'Apparently not. The techs mentioned something about gland secretions still being evident in the prints they lifted. Basically, they were fresh.' Alexander seemed very satisfied with this fact.

'Is it enough to charge him – have any witnesses come forward?'

The DI shook his head. 'We've got the neighbour's testimony sighting an unfamiliar van parked on the street that day, but no outright identification of

Galt's vehicle, which is actually very distinctive. However, the guy has no alibi for the afternoon and evening of the murder. His girlfriend was visiting her family in Dublin.'

'What about the items stolen from the house, any sign of them?'

'Galt works out of an electrical appliances warehouse. We're assuming that's where the TV and stereo system ended up being fenced. Unfortunately, it's very difficult to trace stolen goods once they've been shipped out.'

'So, was the robbery the main motive do you think, or was it getting even with Morna?'

'I suspect that the robbery was always the primary objective, but Galt's relationship with Mrs Murphy complicated matters. Confronting her in that house may not have been part of the plan. He simply lost control. The Fiscal gave us the go-ahead to raise an arrest warrant. I couldn't have found him without your advice Dani, thank you.'

Bevan shrugged off his gratitude. 'Did you look into the possibility that the Murphys had been in the news recently?'

'Yes I did. I couldn't find any reference to Morna, but Lyle is in the local paper a lot. His department send out press releases on a regular basis setting out what he's doing to further the cause of affordable, social housing in Dundee. Lyle is also a frequent contributor to the letters page, where he challenges his detractors. The man *is* a councillor. You would expect him to have a reasonably high public profile. I couldn't identify anything that would have caused him to be more conspicuous than normal over these past few months. I took your suggestion very seriously.' Alexander placed his hand between Dani's shoulder blades, gently leading her back down the slope, in the direction of a cafeteria based in a small wooden hut near to an old band stand.

As the sun disappeared behind the clouds, it became noticeably chillier. Bevan was relieved to enter the building, where the heating was on full blast. She took off her padded jacket and fleece.

'What would you like? They do a mean ice-cream in this place, although it's hardly the season for it.' Alexander smiled.

'I'd love a hot chocolate, please.'

Dani sat at a table by the steamed up window and watched Gordon Alexander place the order. She suddenly imagined him lining up to buy his children an ice-cream cone on a sunny day, after they'd been playing in the park. The thought made her eyes fill up with tears. Bevan had to battle hard to regain her composure.

When he returned, the DI placed a couple of mugs on the scratched Formica surface between them. 'At least they don't add marshmallows here. I've always thought that was a blatant Americanism, quite out of place in a café like this one.'

'I agree,' Dani smiled. 'Although I suspect that most children love having a packet of sweets sprinkled on top of their drink.'

'Yes, they certainly do.' Gordon Alexander took a sip of coffee and looked at his companion closely. 'If you don't mind me saying DCI Bevan, I would have expected somebody like you to have a husband and a couple of kids by now.'

Dani was surprised by his candour. 'Well, you know what it's like on the force, especially for a woman. But that's not really the explanation.' She took a deep breath. 'My mother was very ill after she had me and didn't ever recover. The truth is that I was always frightened of the same thing happening to me.'

Gordon nodded, his deep-set brown eyes full of sadness. 'I can understand that. You were protecting yourself. All I can say, Dani, is that we never quite know what life is going to throw at us, but I would not have been without those few precious years I spent with my wife and children. You shouldn't hold back from having what you really want because you're frightened of losing it. That's no way to live your life.'

Dani knew the man's words were heartfelt and well intentioned. She couldn't possibly take offence. Instead, she reached her hand across the table and laid it over his, giving his large, rough palm a gentle and reassuring squeeze.

*

The Keenes' new extension was progressing well. The foundations were in place and Louise could get a sense of what the finished space would look like. The upheaval caused by the knocking out of the exterior wall was long past and the rest of the house had returned to some semblance of normal.

Col had taken the van to collect some extra supplies from the warehouse, leaving Davy to continue working on the structure of the building. Louise crept out of the kitchen door with a mug of sweet tea. She placed it down on a pile of bricks.

Davy turned his tanned face towards her and smiled. He slipped an arm around her waist and pinned her against the back wall of the house, depositing kisses on her neck and burying his face into the soft contours of her ample breasts.

'Steady on!' She giggled, 'one of the neighbours might see us.'

Without replying Davy scooped Louise up, so that

her legs were wrapped tightly around his body and his arm was hooked under her bottom. He carried her into the house. With a determined and slightly intense look on his face, he continued straight up the stairs to the bedroom.

Chapter 25

As Dani approached DCI Carmichael's office, she could tell that something was going on. There was a palpable buzz of excitement rippling across the incident room. Before she reached the door, DC Webber intercepted her path.

'DCI Bevan, we've had a development.' The younger man led Dani towards his workstation, where several other officers were gathered, including DI Mike Tait. 'I spoke with Rob Wheelan this morning. He told me that eighteen months ago, he and his wife had an extension added to their kitchen.'

Dani immediately recalled the bright, newly fitted area that she'd stood in with Peggy's dad whilst he prepared them tea. She cursed herself for not making the connection sooner.

'It was a local firm who carried out the work,' Webber continued, gesturing towards the screen of his monitor. 'They are a father and son operation. The owner is Gus Bannerman and his son is called Mark.'

One of the officers whistled.

'Did Rob say that Peggy ever came into contact with these men?' Dani enquired, careful that they shouldn't jump the gun.

'Peggy's father claims that she and the twins were always at their house, especially during the pre-school holidays. If they'd had an unsettled night Pat used to give the girls lunch whilst Peggy had a rest. The Wheelans' place was like a second home to

Peggy Fisher.'

'Has anyone paid Mark Bannerman a visit yet?'

'No Ma'am, we were waiting for DCI Carmichael to come back from her meeting.'

Dani considered this for a moment. 'I don't think your DCI would want you to hold back on the lead. DI Tait, can you take us there?'

The man hoisted up his bulky frame and nodded. 'Aye, let's make sure we don't miss the boat this time around.'

*

The Bannerman property was a semi-detached ex-council house on the end of a terrace. A make-shift garage dominated the large side plot and various pieces of rusty equipment were stored beneath an ill-fitting sheet of tarpaulin on the long driveway.

Dani stood well back and allowed Tait and Webber to lead the operation. After banging on the door for several minutes, a small woman with a heavily lined face opened up.

DI Tait held aloft his warrant card. 'Mrs Bannerman? We'd like a word with your son.'

She stood back and allowed them all to enter. The house was dark and the corridor narrow. Bevan found it difficult to imagine how those capable of producing a light and airy extension were prepared to live in such squalor.

Mrs Bannerman led them into a living room which smelt of stale cigarette smoke, but possessed a very pleasant view out across the countryside. 'What do you want with Mark?' She asked bluntly.

'Does he live here with you?' Tait demanded. 'We couldn't find another address for him.'

'Not any longer 'e doesn't.'

'Where is your husband today?'

"E's dead.'

'Oh, I'm terribly sorry.' Mike Tait silently cursed himself. They'd not thought to do a check before they left the headquarters. 'When did Mr Bannerman pass away?'

The woman ducked into the kitchen and came back out with a packet of cigarettes. She lit one before replying, 'it was six months ago. Gus was fitting a new front door for one of our neighbours when he clutched at his chest and turned beetroot. He was dead in minutes. The ambulance didn't reach him for half an hour, not that it would have done any good to arrive sooner.'

'And your son?' Dani prompted.

'I've not seen 'im for over a year. He didn't even come back for his Dad's funeral. Sodding waste of space.'

'Do you have any idea where Mark may have gone?' Alec Webber found himself rapidly losing patience.

'Off with one of his women, Gus said. He took a phone call from Mark. Apparently, this one was serious and he was leaving to set up home with her. Gus didn't really mind too much because Mark was always shagging the clients' wives. He was a bloody liability.'

'And you've heard *nothing* from your son since?' Tait looked incredulous. 'Not a Christmas card or an indication of where he now lives?'

She shrugged her shoulders. 'We weren't the sodding Swiss Family Robinson. There was no money to inherit when Gus fell off 'is perch. I wouldn't expect Mark to be back in touch, there'd be nothing in it for 'im.'

'Have you at least got a photograph of your son?'

She frowned, which made her face criss-cross with a myriad of spidery lines. 'Yeah, I think I've got a couple. I'd like them back mind,' she added sternly.

Dani marvelled at the woman's strangely contradictory behaviour as they waited for her to fetch the snapshots from upstairs.

*

DCI Carmichael didn't appear happy. She was forced to take a back seat to DI Tait during the briefing, because she wasn't up to speed with any of the facts. If looks could have killed, Bevan would be six feet under. But Dani was all too aware that Eric Fisher's trial started in two days. Annie Carmichael's dented pride wasn't really her priority.

Tait was pointing to a photograph pinned to one of the boards. It had been enlarged by the techies. 'We showed this picture to Annette Walker. She identified Mark Bannerman as the person she'd seen with Peggy at the travel agency. I believe we can be confident that he was Peggy Fisher's lover.' Tait took a step forward, warming to the task. 'Mark Ian Bannerman is 36 years old. He is 6'2" in height and of a muscular build. As you can see from his photograph, Mark has light brown hair which, according to his mother, he usually wore to his shoulders.'

'Peggy has been dead now for a year. If Mark took off with a fancy woman, it certainly wasn't her,' Carmichael put in fiercely.

'No, but Mark was a one for the ladies, Ma'am. Either he left with one of his other squeezes sometime before the Fishers' were murdered and is now living happily ever after with her, or it was Mark who killed his lover and her children, going to ground straight afterwards.'

Carmichael sighed bitterly. 'We need to circulate

this photograph and check all the airports, bus stations and ferry terminals to see if Mark Bannerman left the country in the days and weeks following the murders.' She slammed her hand down on the desk in front of her in frustration. 'I'll need to speak with the DCS and the Fiscal's office. With this new information, Eric Fisher might be walking free without even setting foot in the dock.'

Chapter 26

The next few hours seemed to pass painfully slowly. After filling DCS Nicholson in on the latest developments, Bevan decided to leave Annie's team to it. Nicholson was so enraged by the cock-up that he was threatening to pull DCI Carmichael off the case and put Dani on it in her place. Bevan had told him she'd certainly take the investigation over if he wanted her to, but he should give the woman a chance to make amends first.

*

Dani was waiting for news with Sally Irving-Bryant in her mother's kitchen in Leith. It seemed only fitting to be with the person who'd introduced her to the case in the first place whilst they anticipated hearing the fate of Eric Fisher.

Linda Irving got up to prepare their second pot of coffee. 'I still don't entirely understand,' she said. 'Even with this other man having been on the scene, it certainly doesn't mean that Eric Fisher didn't murder his wife and children. It actually provides him with a motive, doesn't it?'

'Yes, but the entire process has been flawed from the very beginning, Mum.' Sally slipped her elegant fingers around a china mug. 'The police investigation failed to pursue crucial leads in the run up to Eric's arrest. If this evidence was available to the Procurator Fiscal back then, Eric may never have been charged. The existence of this person, Mark Bannerman, is too important to be disclosed to the defence team only 48 hours before we get to court.

The Fiscal will either call for a suspension or he'll dismiss the trial altogether.'

'Do you and Eric get any say in the matter?' Dani asked.

'Thankfully, yes. I've submitted a letter setting out the mistakes made by the police and prosecution team as I see them. It also points out how Eric Fisher has spent an *entire year* either on remand in prison or handcuffed to a hospital bed. If the trial is delayed indefinitely, with no guarantee that Bannerman can be located after all this time has passed, then he's been effectively imprisoned for a crime without trial. In a civilised state, we cannot allow this to happen.'

Dani made a mental note that if she ever needed a lawyer, Sally would be the one to call.

Linda came back over with the fresh coffee pot. 'But what if Eric is guilty of killing that woman and those poor children? Is he simply going to walk free?'

Jim Irving entered the room at this moment, wearing a casual shirt and jeans. 'If that is the case, darling, then it's the police who are to blame. Their total ineptitude has caused this case to collapse.'

Linda shot Dani an embarrassed glance.

'Mr Irving is right. The original investigating team were far too narrow in their approach. They had Eric Fisher as a prime suspect from the start and refused to widen the inquiry to look at the lives of Peggy and the children. The victims are usually the first people we consider in a homicide case.'

'How did it go so badly wrong?' Jim took a chair next to the DCI and helped himself to a cup of coffee. The ex-lawyer was clearly very interested to know.

'I believe it was because the SIO was sidetracked by the concept of family annihilation. She brought in an advisor from the States who pushed the team down a very defined path. Don't get me wrong, I can see exactly how it happened. The murder scene made the case appear clear-cut. But a detective must never close their mind to other possibilities, however far-fetched they may seem.'

Jim nodded sagely.

Bevan turned towards Sally, determined to change the subject. 'Did you know that Grant's company are restoring an old bothy not far from my dad's place on Colonsay?'

'Yes, I do recall him mentioning something. It's a lovely spot.'

Dani edged forward. 'You see, the bothy lies on the edge of a clan battle site. There's a historic cairn positioned within the area designated for development. My father and some of the local residents would really like to meet with Grant, so that they can discuss the issue with him. Then, they might be able to reach a compromise without having to get the planners involved again.'

Sally appeared disconcerted. It was clear she didn't often find herself drawn into her husband's business affairs. 'Oh – I'm really not sure -' she stammered. Their awkward discussion was halted by the trilling of Sally's mobile phone. She lifted it out of her pocket and listened in silence.

The others waited expectantly.

Sally ended the call and laid the phone down carefully on the table. Her expression was unreadable. 'That was the Fiscal's office. All charges against my client have been dropped. Eric Fisher will be released later on today.'

Chapter 27

'Does Sally Irving-Bryant know where he'll go?' Andy Calder asked, in a neutral tone.

'The house in Dalkeith is still leased to Eric. But I can't see him going back there in a hurry, not when people think he's most likely got off on a technicality. Sally has advised him to rent a flat in the city, somewhere anonymous. He should receive compensation for the period he spent in prison, although it will be several months before he sees any of it.'

Andy tutted. 'I'm not sure I agree with him getting money from the tax-payer. His innocence hasn't *actually* been proved.'

'And whose fault is that?' Dani snapped.

'Those numpties at City and Borders,' he responded, quick as a flash.

She sighed heavily. 'It's a real shame. They're going to get crucified by the internal review board. I feel sorry for Annie.'

Calder raised his eyebrows, indicating he thought her sympathy was misplaced.

Dani glanced at her watch, noting it was nearly six. 'Why don't you head off home? You can catch Amy before she goes to bed.'

A shadow fell across the man's face. 'Yeah, I suppose so.'

'Have you spoken to Carol yet – about the stuff you mentioned the other day?'

'No. To be honest, I'm not really looking forward to shattering my wife's every hope and dream.'

'It may not actually be as serious as that. You won't know until you talk to her.' Dani stood up and opened her office door. She strode across to Calder's work station and retrieved his jacket, returning to hand it to him. 'Off you go. Pick up some flowers on the way home and have a proper conversation over dinner.'

He took the crumpled jacket and pulled it on, grunting something inaudible before shuffling away towards the lift, looking like a man resigned to his fate.

*

A band of fierce weather had battered the west coast of Colonsay for a week. During these inclement periods, Huw Bevan tended to hunker down in his bungalow and wait it out. He was an obsessive follower of the radio forecast and always knew when a stormy patch was due. This meant he could stock up on food and fuel in the village well in advance.

On this particular morning, the clouds had finally lifted, revealing a welcome shimmer of gold that lingered along the horizon. Huw went immediately to the kitchen and roused Gill from his basket, grabbing the lead and pulling on boots and a coat before the favourable conditions had an opportunity to change.

Gill practically dragged his master across the field towards the beach. Huw released the dog from its lead and was required to pick up a brisk pace in order to keep the animal in sight. They were heading rapidly towards Jilly O'Keefe's place. As Huw drew closer, he could make out some kind of disturbance taking place up the hillside.

The developers had been nowhere near the bothy whilst the weather was so awful. Something told

Huw that today they must be back. He whistled to Gill, who returned to his side at a sprint. Slipping the lead back on, they proceeded in the direction of all the commotion.

The vision which greeted Huw almost made him laugh out loud, until he saw the trickle of blood on his neighbour's forehead.

'What on earth is happening here?' He demanded, marching to the top of a grassy hillock, where Jilly O'Keefe was standing in front of a mini-digger. The rumbling piece of machinery was attempting to shift the pile of stones which constituted the Macfie cairn.

A big bruiser of a man leapt out of the cab. 'This old boot threw herself in front of my bucket. She's damned lucky to still be alive.'

Jilly crossed her arms over her chest defiantly, her white hair blowing in the breeze. 'You have no right to destroy this ancient monument. Its preservation is currently the matter of a legal appeal.'

Huw wasn't sure this was strictly true.

'It's the first I've heard of it darlin',' the man bawled over the sound of the engine. 'I'm just here to do my job, pal,' he said to Huw. 'As far as I've been told, the planners have signed off on everything.'

Huw raised his arms, trying to calm the situation down a little. 'The plans were agreed before anyone knew the significance of this place. Can I ask you to delay your clearance of the area, just until I've had a chance to make a few phone calls?'

The burly man put a hand up to his stubbly chin and scratched. 'Och, I don't know about that...'

Huw took a step nearer, observing his face more closely. '*Dougie Beath*?'

The digger driver shifted about awkwardly. 'Aye, that's right, what of it?'

'Don't you recognise me, lad?' Huw asked in a more strident voice. 'I'm Mr Bevan.'

The man stood up a little straighter. 'Sorry, I didnae realise it was you, sir.'

'Not to worry. It's been a long time. Your family moved to Oban didn't they? What brings you back here?'

'I've been working for Bryant Construction this last five years. I travel to places all over Scotland. This is the first time I've been back to the island, though.'

'Well, may I suggest that the three of us take a walk over to my house? It isn't far. I'll brew a pot of tea and light the fire, then we can discuss this matter like civilised folk.'

'Okay,' Dougie said sheepishly, leaning into the cab and turning off the engine.

'Now,' Huw continued, 'I think you owe Mrs O'Keefe an apology. I wouldn't like to think that those good manners we instilled in you as a wee boy have all gone astray. I don't believe for a moment that's true.'

'No, you're right, Mr Bevan, I'll be sure to do that at once, sir.'

Chapter 28

It was just a short walk from the Bankfoot Arms to Kenneth Macallan's house. He'd only had a couple of pints but felt a little wobbly on his feet. Then he remembered. One of his clients at the garage had bought him a dram in between. Ken was getting worried about the amount of little details that'd been slipping his mind recently. If he wasn't careful, he was going to climb behind the wheel after having one too many. It would be disastrous to lose your licence in Ken's line of business.

It was dark, and along this thin stretch of the Dunkeld Road there were no lights. The Macallans' place was in the centre of a Victorian terrace, running along the southerly route out of the village, towards Perth. Ken fumbled to fit his key inside the lock. When the door finally opened, he nearly fell with it into the hallway.

Finding his footing again the man carefully took off his coat and cap, placing them on the hook next to his wife's woollen jacket. Without his outer garments on the house felt cold. Nancy must have already gone to bed and let the fire go out, he decided.

Believing his wife was upstairs, Ken thought there'd be no harm in fixing himself a wee snifter of single malt. He shuffled into the living room and headed straight for the drinks cabinet, without bothering to switch on the light.

As Ken unscrewed the bottle, a sudden rush of cold air made the hairs on the back of his neck stand up. He shivered, pouring out the liquid as swiftly as he could and taking a swig, feeling it pleasantly burning his mouth and throat. He slowly turned, to see that one of the small windows had been left open. The man was puzzled. Nancy was always very careful about locking the place up at night.

He walked across the room with a sigh, reaching up to pull it closed and securing the sneck at the bottom. Ken stood for a moment and had another sip from the glass, staring out into the darkness, immediately wondering why the outside light wasn't on. It was one of those automatic ones, which came to life as soon as the sun went down. The only explanation he could come up with was that the bulb had died, even though the ironmonger told him it would keep going for fifteen years. Ken nearly laughed out loud. The poxy thing hadn't lasted six months.

In that moment, the smile that had half formed on his lips faded. In the blackness of the glass, Ken could see the dimly lit corridor leading to the front door reflected back at him. In the centre of it stood a tall figure, dressed entirely in black. Ken let the tumbler slip from his grasp and land on the carpet with a dull thud. He watched in horror as the figure began to advance, raising something aloft in its right hand.

Kenneth was too terrified to shift around and face this monster so he stood absolutely still, with his eyes screwed tight shut. Until he felt the sudden assault of blows, which seemed to be raining down on his back and shoulders, delivered with such a rage that the man felt as if he'd somehow brought the wrath of God down upon himself.

Ken's legs finally buckled. His body collapsed forwards, crashing through the thin pane of glass to collapse lifeless amongst the dozens of tiny shards which coated the paving slabs below.

*

Dani glanced through the window of the café on Royal Exchange Square before she entered. DCI Annie Carmichael was already in there, dressed in a smart, dark suit and looking in every respect as if she were on her way to a funeral.

Bevan pushed through the door and weaved past the tables to join her. Annie already had a cup of jet black liquid clutched in her hands.

'Thanks so much for agreeing to meet me, Dani.'

'Not at all, when's your appointment?' Bevan knew that DCI Carmichael was due to meet with the internal review board at the Pitt Street Headquarters some time that day.

'3pm this afternoon.' The woman gave a wry smile. 'The last time I was at Pitt Street was to receive a bravery award. You're only as good as your last case, eh?'

'But the Fisher case isn't over yet, Annie. There's still a chance to turn this situation around. Have you had any luck tracing Mark Bannerman?'

She shifted up a little higher in her seat. 'We're fairly certain that Mark didn't leave the country, not unless he was able to get hold of false papers of some kind. My hunch is that he's still in the UK. We've circulated his photograph and called for him to surrender himself to the authorities voluntarily, so that we can *eliminate him from our enquiries.*'

'How about doing a piece on Crime Scotland? Television appeals have to be very visual in nature, but you've got his mother's photographs. You might find somebody out there who recognises him.'

Annie looked interested. 'Aye, that's a good idea.

We could make it sound as if we're concerned about his welfare. That may make his ladyfriend more likely to come forward.'

Dani gratefully received a cappuccino from the young waitress. 'You can mention your plans at the review panel this afternoon. Let them know that you're not beaten just yet.'

Carmichael leant across and placed her hand over Dani's. 'I know that you asked Nicholson to allow me to keep control of the case. I appreciate it. You didn't have to do that.'

'There aren't that many of us women in high-ranking positions. It certainly doesn't help matters if we don't fight each other's corner when times are tough.'

The woman removed her hand and smiled. 'Well, I owe you one.' She slowly sipped the bitter liquid, the sharp taste almost making her grimace. 'Do you believe that this Mark Bannerman guy was the one who killed Peggy and the children? Was there really an intruder in the Fishers' home that Sunday afternoon?'

Bevan took several minutes to answer. 'I don't know Annie. I honestly don't know.'

Chapter 29

Grant Bryant didn't visit his building sites very often these days, preferring to delegate that job to his site managers. But he'd received a strange request from one of his employees. When he mentioned it to his wife, she told him that the issue had something to do with the father of her DCI friend. Sally had told him to take it seriously otherwise her brother would be cross with them.

So here he was, at the helipad on the Isle of Colonsay. Bryant saw Dougie Beath approaching in one of their company 4x4s. He pulled the vehicle up beside his boss, jumping out to open the passenger door for him.

'It's only a couple of miles up the road, sir,' he explained. 'I told Mr Bevan that we'd meet at his place. It's actually very pleasant.'

Bryant nodded, amazed to see the usually taciturn and brutish Beath being so well mannered and communicative. He wondered what on earth had come over the man, whom he had employed purely because he worked like a carthorse, not for his diplomatic skills.

But Beath was right. Bevan's bungalow was spacious and well maintained, with a stunning view out across a beautiful, sandy shore and towards the seemingly endless span of the Atlantic Ocean. Bryant noticed a framed photograph of DCI Dani Bevan taking pride of place on the mantelpiece and could immediately identify a resemblance in the features of the lean, grey-haired man stood before him.

'Thank you for coming all this way to speak with us,' Huw Bevan began, gesturing for Grant to take a seat next to a cosy wood-burning stove.

The businessman then noticed an unkempt woman sitting in the armchair opposite. She wore a kind of multi-coloured knitted smock finished off with a pair of sturdy black boots.

'This is Jilly O'Keefe,' Huw continued. 'She owns the cottage just adjacent to your development.'

Grant nodded politely to the woman, whose expression remained steely. He sincerely hoped that Bevan wasn't going to leave him alone with this lady. Luckily, his host settled into the seat beside her.

Not usually rattled by much, Grant was forced to perform a double-take as Dougie re-entered the large living room carrying a tray of teas and coffees, which he'd apparently prepared himself, without any evident prompting. The man set the drinks down on the table and sloped off into another room, to let the rest of them talk in peace.

'Now, what can I do to help?' Grant beamed broadly and displayed his palms in an open gesture.

'It has come to our attention,' Huw stated, 'that your building work is set to destroy a very important ancient monument. It is one of the few surviving cairns of the clan Macfie left on Colonsay, the rest having been destroyed by the elements or the sea. It would seem rather crass to bulldoze such an important artefact of our Scottish heritage.'

'I see,' Grant commented, nodding his head gravely. 'I'm afraid this 'monument' is not catalogued in the deeds that accompany the land. I had no problems in receiving the appropriate planning permissions from the council.'

Jilly O'Keefe snorted loudly.

Ignoring the interruption, Huw explained, 'it is a

cairn known to the locals of the island but has perhaps never been officially recorded. I'm afraid that much of what goes on in remote communities such as ours is carried forward through word-of-mouth and folklore. Working as you do in many out-of-the-way places like this, you are surely sensitive to such cultural differences. We aren't in the centre of Glasgow here, Mr Bryant.' Huw softened the sting in his words by pouring milk into one of the mugs and handing it to his guest.

Grant thought about this. He did very occasionally have to tweak his plans on a conversion because of certain local idiosyncrasies. His eyes strayed to the woman in the armchair, who was training upon him a look of undisguised hatred. It didn't do to stoke up animosity. He turned back to his host. 'Sally informs me that your daughter was a tremendous help with her last case. So I tell you what, after we've finished our tea, you can take me for a walk along the shore. I'd like to look at this ancient cairn for myself.'

Huw picked up one of the mugs and settled back into his armchair, with a satisfied smile on his face.

*

DS Phil Boag knocked on the door of Bevan's office, entering when he caught his boss's eye.

'What is it, Phil?' Dani hadn't been able to help but notice that since the end of his marriage several months back, her detective sergeant looked like a changed man. He was toned and healthy and had a noticeable spring in his step.

'Have you read the bulletin yet, Ma'am?'

'No?'

Phil strode inside and took the chair opposite. 'There's some news in it from central division. A couple in Bankfoot were attacked in their home during a burglary. Both are dead.'

'*Shit*. When did this happen?'

'I don't know all the details yet, Ma'am. The bodies were discovered a couple of days ago, I think. Would you like me to find out more?'

'Aye, I certainly would. But in the meantime, I need to go one better than that.'

*

Andy Calder drove his boss straight to the scene. A Victorian terraced property had been entirely sealed off from the road. Several squad cars lined the narrow street. Dani was heartened to spot a face she recognised amongst the plain-clothed detectives gathered in the front garden. DS Dave Driscoll. They'd worked together on a case a couple of years back. Bevan knew he was a decent copper.

The man turned towards the detectives as they marched up the path. 'DCI Bevan,' he declared with a warm smile. 'Good to see you again.'

Dani shook his hand firmly. 'Is the SIO inside?'

'Aye,' Dave replied gravely. 'The crime scene suits are there by the door if you want to go in.'

'Can you fill Andy in on the details?' Dani asked matter-of-factly, leaving the pair to it and swiftly pulling on one of the ungainly plastic overalls.

The entrance way was poky and dark. Bevan glanced around her as she proceeded towards the sitting room at the back. This was where the techies were hard at work. There was barely anywhere to stand in the cramped space. A tall man, with a mask covering his face stepped gingerly towards her. 'DCI Bevan?' He enquired.

She nodded. 'What have we got here, DI Hawthorn?'

'The bodies were removed late last night.' He

turned to point at the gap where a window had once been. 'During or after the attack, Kenneth Macallan, 58 years old, went crashing through the glass and ended up on the patio. He'd received multiple stab wounds to the back and shoulders from a long-blade knife of some description. Nancy Macallan was stabbed in her bed. Preliminary examinations suggest she may have been asleep during the assault.'

'Where were the knife wounds positioned on Nancy's body?'

Hawthorn indicated the areas on his own torso. 'The majority were to her back and side. We assume that she was lying, facing away from the bedroom door when the killer struck.'

'Any sign of the murder weapon?'

'Not so far, Ma'am. I've got officers doing a sweep search up the hillside at the rear. The intruder got in through the kitchen door. The neighbour says the Macallans kept a spare key under a plant pot in the garden.'

'For heaven's sake,' Dani muttered. 'I expect it took him about five minutes to locate the thing.'

'The security light outside has been smashed. It looks like he made off with a cash box. According to one of Macallan's employees, it contained the day's taking from the garage he ran in the centre of the village. It was a few hundred pounds, max.'

'It doesn't seem a great deal for two lives.'

'We're hoping to lift prints from somewhere in the house, but the chances are the perpetrator was wearing gloves.'

'Are you aware of the Murphy murder in Dundee?' Dani asked.

'Aye, I followed it on the news. The woman there was stabbed too, wasn't she?'

'Multiple stab wounds to the back and shoulders.

Just like Kenneth Macallan. I strongly recommend that you give DI Gordon Alexander a call. He's in charge of the case. There are strong indications here that we may be looking at the same attacker in both instances.'

'But haven't they got someone in custody for the Dundee murder?'

Dani nodded. 'Since when has that been any guarantee that the guy was guilty?'

Hawthorn chuckled. 'I'll get on to Alexander as soon as we return to the station.' The man lowered his voice. 'You realise that this may mean we have some kind of serial offender on our hands?'

'Yes,' Dani said carefully. 'I do.'

Chapter 30

Bevan led the way back to Calder's car, her mobile phone clamped to her ear. 'So when *exactly,* was the guy released?' She demanded. 'Okay, well thanks for your help, Sally.'

Dani climbed into the passenger seat and closed the door, waiting for Andy to join her. 'Fisher's been out of prison for five days,' she said flatly. 'He could have done this.'

'But he couldn't have killed Morna Murphy,' Andy replied, turning the vehicle round in the middle of the road and heading back in the direction of Perth.

'No,' Dani replied softly, staring out of the window at the lush, green fields. 'What about Mark Bannerman? He's been out there somewhere for over a year. If he was the one who murdered the Fishers, then these other killings could be down to him, too.'

'But why wait so long before striking again and then murdering twice within such a short space of time? It doesn't make any sense.'

Bevan turned to look at her companion. 'What if Bannerman was living in another part of the country up until recently. Maybe he's only come back to east Scotland in the last few months.'

'Or perhaps the Fisher case generated so much publicity that he had to lie low. If Bannerman wanted Eric Fisher to get the blame for the murders, then he'd have to rein himself in for as long as possible, otherwise it would be obvious to the world that it wasn't an incidence of family annihilation at all.'

'Of course,' Dani replied with feeling. 'Whoever

killed Peggy and the children would have to suppress any urge they had to do it again. But after nearly a year of waiting, the man couldn't control himself any longer and he started killing once more.'

Andy was about to say something but stopped.

'What is it?'

He shrugged his shoulders, keeping his vision fixed on the winding road ahead. 'I don't know. It's a bit far-fetched.'

'Go on, we need to consider everything.'

'Well, what if these break-ins across the eastern region have something to do with this? Perhaps Bannerman had to find other ways to release his urges. It might have been like the next best thing. Sorry, it sounds a bit weird to say it out loud.'

Dani furrowed her brow in thought. 'Can we take a detour on the way back?'

'Sure, Ma'am, where are we headed?'

'To see a couple of old friends.'

*

Bill Hutchison appeared surprised but pleased to see the two officers. 'Do come in,' he said eagerly. 'Joy is out shopping in town, I'm afraid.'

'That's okay. We won't disturb you for long.'

Andy put out his hand to the older man. 'I'm glad to have the opportunity to see you again, Bill,' Calder said. 'I've wanted to tell you how impressed I was with the way you sprung that prostitution racket. You've got more balls than most men on the force. I'm not exaggerating, either. We've got so many box tickers these days you wouldn't believe.'

Bill sighed. 'What Detective Sharpe and I did wasn't really enough, if truth be told. There must be hundreds more girls still in that awful predicament.'

They were led into the sunny lounge, where Dani

took a seat on the sofa.

'You can't afford to start thinking that way, Bill.' Calder laid a hand on the man's shoulder. 'It'll drive you round the twist. Just be satisfied with the small changes you were able to make.'

'Can I offer you both a spot of afternoon tea?'

'That won't be necessary, thank you.' Dani shifted forward. 'Did you have any more ideas about the local burglaries – do you know if the police have come up with any suspects yet?'

'They've certainly not made any arrests. But I *have* done a little bit of digging myself, yes.' Bill rested his weight on the arm of a chair.

Dani waited patiently for her friend to continue.

'Joy and I invited some of the neighbours round for drinks last weekend. We took the opportunity to ask them a few questions.'

'Nice cover.' Andy nodded his head, looking impressed.

'What we ascertained was that a couple of the houses which were broken into *had* used that carpet cleaning company recently – the one that Rita employed.' Bill cleared his throat and looked sheepish. 'So Joy and I booked an appointment with them ourselves. They came to do the work yesterday.'

Dani sat bolt upright, but couldn't help glancing at the soft, beige pile beneath her feet, thinking what a good job they'd done. 'What did you do that for, Bill? These men could be extremely dangerous!'

'Well, our theory was so speculative, that I felt the local detectives wouldn't be interested. Also, when our grandsons were here for the weekend, they did make a terrible mess by the back door.'

'What did you make of them?' Calder asked with interest, ignoring his boss's reservations and Bill's comments on the house's domestic upkeep.

'We found the two men who came to be efficient and rather charming. There was an older chap by the name of Oliver and his nephew, Dean.'

Andy reached into the pocket of his jacket and pulled out the photograph of Mark Bannerman. 'This was taken a couple of years back. Could this person be one of the men who came to your house yesterday?'

Bill examined the image very closely. He shook his head. 'No, Detective Constable Calder, that man isn't the right age. I'd say that Oliver was in his forties and Dean in his twenties. The individual in your photograph is somewhere between the two.'

'When you spoke with the neighbours, did any of them say they'd come into contact with the person who broke into their property – was there violence of any kind involved?' Dani asked.

'No, the break-ins tended to occur when the householders were out, as one would expect with a burglary. Most criminals do not wish to come face-to-face with the person they are robbing. It increases their chances of getting caught. A burglar who gets discovered in the house hasn't done their job properly.'

'Unless the point of breaking in wasn't actually to steal stuff,' Calder put in dryly.

'But what else could it be?' Bill asked innocently.

'What else indeed,' Dani replied.

'Now, let me at least fetch you a cold drink. Joy will be home soon and she'd love to see you both. So you really can't go dashing off without taking refreshment of some kind.'

Chapter 31

A strong wind was whipping across the golden sands, but thankfully, it was at their backs as the three walkers proceeded along the shore to the cairn.

Huw had to admit that the jumble of stones looked a little pathetic, standing as it did on the edge of a messy building site. The machinery sat motionless around it, like a group of inanimate worshippers at the foot of a sacred monument.

Jilly climbed the mound ahead of them, carefully picking up the loose stones and attempting to reassemble the structure as best she could.

Grant Bryant strode briskly around the hillock, closely observing the scene. 'It's certainly a cairn. I'm amazed that the landowner never mentioned its existence on this spot when the property was sold to us.'

'I believe the folk who passed on the property to you didn't know the island at all well. The bothy and its garden were all part of a bequest. One that was obviously unwanted.'

'Why were the Macfie clan so important to the history of Colonsay?'

Huw was surprised by Bryant's apparent interest. 'The Macfies are one of the oldest of the Scottish clans. Colonsay is their ancestral home. The family was understood to have a mystical connection to this place. That is why the landmarks associated with the clan have always been so special to the islanders. In 1623, the last of the Macfie Chiefs was tied to a standing stone over at Balaruminmore and shot. After that point, the clan were dispersed and the Macdonalds ruled in their place.'

Bryant nodded, turning to gaze out to sea, where the brisk breeze was making it difficult for the clouds to congregate for long. He could just make out the distant outline of the coast of Donegal, where his own family had originated from. 'How about I take another look through those plans,' he called over to the retired headmaster. 'I'm sure we can shift around the boundaries a little, in order to preserve this piece of the island's history. Maybe there would be a story in it, for the local paper, I mean? We could make a feature of the cairn. Help to preserve it properly for the future. So that others might be able to enjoy its simple beauty. The publicity could be very beneficial to us all.'

Catching the businessman's drift straight away, Huw strode across the churned up earth and put out his hand to Grant. The man shook it firmly.

'You've got a deal,' Huw pronounced.

'Now, have you got any whisky back at that house of yours?' Bryant wrapped his arms around his chest, feeling the merciless bite of the southerly wind.

'Aye. I might even be persuaded to get out my single malt.'

'Just lead the way,' Grant responded with a smile.

'Jilly! Are you coming back to my place for a wee dram to celebrate?'

'Of course, Huw,' the woman shouted down to her friend and neighbour, from a precarious position halfway up the hillside. 'Do you need to even ask?'

Chapter 32

All that Louise Keene could hear was the tweeting of the birds outside her bedroom window. She glanced at the digital clock. There was forty five minutes before she needed to go and pick up the boys from school.

Louise sat up and reached for her bra and pants, from where they'd been discarded on the floor a couple of hours earlier. She decided to take a shower later, when the boys were back and settled in front of the TV. Once Louise had pulled on her jeans and sweater she padded into the en-suite bathroom and washed her face, observing the pinkish glow that radiated from her cheeks. The woman couldn't help but smile. She'd not felt so bloody good in years.

Downstairs, Davy had put on the kettle and was sitting at the kitchen table, examining the contents of the package that had arrived that morning. Louise placed her arms around his shoulders and brushed her lips across his soft, wavy hair.

'Who's this?' Davy asked, indicating the young boy in the photographs that were spilling out of the pack.

'It's my brother, Neil.'

Davy looked puzzled. 'He's very young.'

'This picture was taken thirty years ago. He died when he was ten years old, in a walking accident. The weather closed in when his class were on a school trip. Three of the children got lost and died of hypothermia.'

The man clasped her hand and pulled her onto

his lap. 'God. I'm really sorry.'

'It was a very long time ago.' Louise scooped up one of the prints. 'Mum wanted some copies made of this picture. It's her favourite. You know, I hadn't realised before how much Ben and Jamie resemble their uncle. Not until I looked at this photo more carefully. I think that must be a comfort to my parents.'

Davy nuzzled his face into her neck. 'Yes, I believe it must be too.'

'Now, come on,' she said affectionately. 'Let's have a quick cuppa. Then I really need to go and fetch the boys.'

*

Gordon Alexander led Dani towards his desk, which was as immaculately tidy as ever.

'DI Hawthorn told me you'd viewed the crime scene in Bankfoot. What did you think? You are the one who's seen them both.'

Bevan narrowed her eyes. 'In the Murphys' case, it was obviously an organised burglary. A wide screen television and lots of electrical equipment was taken. A vehicle had to be involved and it needed to be pre-meditated. Yet with the Macallan murders, there was an element of opportunism to it. Someone found the key to the back door and stole a cash box. Kenneth Macallan had been in the pub that night. I could imagine some local lad spotting him in there and knowing the house would be easy pickings.'

'This person may also have been aware that Kenneth took the cash box from the garage home with him at night. Or that they kept the key under a flowerpot,' Alexander added.

'Exactly. But then why the murders?' Dani shuffled forward in her seat. 'I think we need to ignore the burglary element altogether and simply consider these attacks as homicides. In which case, I think we're looking at a serial offender. So, where does that leave Tommy Galt?'

'We've still got him in custody. The fingerprints are the strongest evidence we have in the Murphy inquiry. I'm almost positive it was Galt who stole the electrical goods.'

'But did he kill Morna, that's the question?'

Gordon Alexander knitted his hands together on the desk in front of him. 'I'm beginning to wonder if we may be looking for an accomplice. Two men working this together perhaps, what do you think?'

Dani nodded. 'It's a solid theory. Tommy Galt is the burglar and someone else does the killing. Only this other individual has developed too much of a taste for the job and is prepared to go it alone, even if Galt is convicted.'

'But surely Galt could be persuaded to name this other man? Especially of it might mean a reduced sentence.'

'Perhaps,' Bevan said carefully. 'But it all depends upon who this person is and what kind of hold he exerts over his associates. The man is obviously a ruthless killer with no mercy.'

Alexander looked troubled. 'I'm going to speak with Tommy Galt once more. He's staring at a life sentence. There *must* be a way of getting him to talk.'

*

The man sitting before them looked broken. His hair was greasy and he'd lost quite a bit of weight. Dani wondered if the police doctor had taken a look at him. Galt immediately struck her as a suicide risk.

Alexander rattled his chair noisily as he sat down. The sound seemed to cause Galt physical pain.

'Do you understand the evidence we have against you Tommy?' The DI began, not unkindly. 'We can place you at the house on the day that Morna was murdered. Yet you swore you'd not been there in months. The forensic proof is unequivocal.'

Galt hung his head. 'Lisa's finished with me. I got a letter a couple of days ago. She took all my gear to the tip.'

'You've got more to worry about than that, Tommy. As it stands, you are going to spend the rest of your life in prison.' Alexander laid his hands flat on the table between them. 'Now, this is how I see it. *You* stake out the properties and work out what's worth stealing, whilst you're working on a place. If one of the wives catches your fancy, then you seduce her at the same time. This helps you to gain easy access. But there's no way you can handle the break-in by yourself. There's got to be somebody who assists you with this part of the operation. He's the muscle man.' Quite unexpectedly, Alexander banged his palms down hard on the table, causing Galt to jolt upright in his seat. 'I believe it was *this* man who killed Morna. Am I right?'

Tommy shook his head. Tears and snot were dripping from his face. 'I don't know who killed her.'

Dani fished in her bag for a packet of tissues. She pulled one out and handed it to Galt. 'What did you find when you got to the house that day, Tommy? We've got your fingerprints on the bedroom doorway. We know you were there.'

'I didn't think Morna would be in. I'd called her the day before to check. We still saw one another every so often, you see. Just for sex. I felt bad, because the intention was always to do the place over. Trade had been really slow since Christmas. The Murphys had the most expensive electrical equipment I'd ever seen in a house in Dundee. But it was complicated, because I really did have feelings for Morna.'

'So you called her up. What did she say?' Dani sat forward and watched his face closely.

'I asked if she wanted to meet me at a hotel. Morna said she couldn't because she was on a training day for work. Morna claimed she'd be in Forfar until late that evening. When I found this out, I knew it was the opportunity I'd been looking for.' Tommy scrunched up the tissue and then opened it out again. 'The shop I work out of has a plain black van. I borrowed that one. I parked up on the Murphys' street and watched the place for a while. It was dead quiet. I approached the house and slipped down the side passage. That's when I saw that the kitchen door had been forced open. I went inside, trying not to touch anything. The place was so eerily quiet that I knew whoever had broken in wasn't still there. For some reason, I walked straight up the stairs. When I reached the bedroom and saw Morna lying there, on the bed, I must have put out a hand to steady myself, although I don't recall doing it. I knew she was dead. There wouldn't have been anything I could have done to save her.'

'You don't actually know that,' Alexander seethed. 'You could at least have called an ambulance for the woman.'

Galt raised his gaze for the first time. 'You don't understand. There was so much blood.'

'What did you do then?' Dani prompted.

'So many thoughts were going through my head. I must have stood in that doorway for at least twenty minutes. But Morna was gone and I'd promised this guy the goods...'

'So you went back downstairs and cleaned the place out - with Morna Murphy lying butchered in her own bedroom.' Dani kept her breathing even.

'I finally pulled myself together and put on my gloves. Then I proceeded to remove all the expensive stuff from the Murphys' house, piece by piece. When I'd filled the van I drove off. I knew that Lyle would be back from work at some point. He would find his wife and know what to do next. I had to think about me and Lisa. We had a wedding to plan and, you know, these things cost the earth.'

Chapter 33

'Did you believe his story?' Andy Calder asked.

'Yes I did. The tale had a sort of tragic banality to it that rang true. I reckon Morna Murphy told Tommy Galt she was on a training day as an excuse, because she didn't fancy having sex with him. This idea never crossed Galt's mind. As she'd initiated sex in the first place, he probably thought she was always up for it.'

'That's the way most men think, yeah,' Calder conceded. 'So without the burglary element, we're simply looking for a cold-blooded killer.'

'In which case, I don't believe we can rule out the idea that Morna had another man on the go. This would also explain why she gave Galt the brush off.'

Phil appeared in the office doorway. 'Can I come in?'

'Of course.'

He leant against the partition. 'I've been looking into the background of the Macallan family. Kenneth Macallan had run the Bankfoot Garage for thirty years. He took it over from his father. The couple have one son, who emigrated to Australia with his wife fifteen years ago. Nancy Macallan taught at the primary school part-time.'

'The family were well known locally, then.' Dani tapped her pen on the desk. 'Who the hell would want to kill them? In Morna's case, I can see how she might have attracted the attention of some psycho by choosing to sleep with the wrong guy. But the Macallans?'

'Neither of the victims had any convictions,' Phil continued. 'DI Hawthorn questioned the landlord of the pub, who said that Kenneth enjoyed a drink. But their house was only a short walk away. He wasn't drinking and driving.'

'Let's hope he was utterly inebriated when that bastard stabbed him to death,' Calder commented evenly.

Dani looked thoughtful. 'But the couple *were* well known in the area. Kenneth ran the garage and Nancy worked at the school.' She had an idea. 'I wonder if either of them had been in the papers recently. Could you check that out for me, Phil?'

'Sure.' The DS turned to leave before adding, 'how's Gordon?'

'He's fine. I've really enjoyed working with him. I like a copper who's open to new ideas.'

'I'm glad he's managing okay. The guy was a total mess after his family had the accident, as you can imagine. I thought he might not return to the force. He blamed himself for not being there with them when the car was hit. For a while, he was resentful of what being a policeman had taken away from him.'

'The work seems to do him good now. It must provide him with some kind of purpose.'

'Gordon can be a bit stiff, but he's got principles.'

'Yes, I've already noticed that.' Dani smiled as Phil returned to his desk.

When he was out of earshot, Andy said, 'Mr Boag could almost have been talking about himself there.'

'Hardly. Phil's not rigid.'

'Don't get me wrong, Ma'am, I like the guy, and actually, he's loosened up a hell of a lot since splitting up with Jane.'

Dani would have to admit this was certainly true. The Boags must have experienced the most civilised divorce in history. Phil had remained in the family home with their two teenage girls and Jane was currently living with Phil's parents in Newton Mearns. It was close to the secondary school where Jane was the Headmistress. There hadn't seemed any point in paying to run two households. This arrangement appeared to suit everyone for the time being. Jane's job had always been the priority for her.

Dani cleared her throat. 'How are things at home? Are Carol and Amy well?'

'You mean, have I had that chat with Carol yet?'

'Actually, yes.'

'We broached the subject the other evening over dinner. I told Carol I wasn't prepared to change my meds. I said that I needed to be around for her and Amy in the long term.'

'How did she react?'

'She agreed. Carol doesn't want me to damage my health.'

'Great, that's the response you wanted, isn't it?' Dani looked at her friend, he didn't exactly seem overjoyed.

'Yeah, it is. But I was watching her later, whilst she was tucking Amy up in bed, when Carol didn't know I was there. She looked sad, Dani. I got a glimpse of how my wife *really* feels and it wasn't good.'

Dani shook her head. 'You've got it wrong. Carol is allowed to be sad sometimes. I promise you, she knows the value of what she's got.'

'But what if Carol always regrets not having another child? I don't know if I can carry that guilt.'

'Listen, what your wife is going through now is a transition. It's like a kind of grief. You need to allow her to come to terms with the decision. Don't expect her to turn bloody somersaults over it, but gradually her grief will fade. Everyone feels sad, Andy, it's a natural part of life and we're perfectly able to live with it. What my mother had was something quite different. Just remember that. You, Carol and Amy are going to have a perfectly happy life. I happen to know that's true.'

Totally unexpectedly, Andy stepped forward and put his arms around his boss, eliciting some amazed glances from the officers working on the floor outside. He squeezed her gently. 'You're right. I'm going to make damn sure they're happy.' Andy released his grip and levered Dani away from him slightly, so that he could look her in the eye. 'Now Ma'am, all we need to do is find someone who can make you happy too.'

Chapter 34

Bill hadn't exactly told DCI Bevan and DC Calder everything when they'd called round the other day. Bill and Joy had done a little bit more than just ask questions about the burglaries that had been plaguing their estate, they'd also come up with a plan.

Whilst the carpet cleaning men were carrying out their job at the Hutchisons' house, between the two of them, they'd managed to disclose certain false details. They informed Oliver and Dean that the burglar alarm had been playing up and they'd had to disconnect it, that they'd recently bought a brand new television set and that the pair of them would be leaving for a mini-break in Paris the following Wednesday.

Right at this moment, Bill and Joy were sitting on stools in front of Rita McCulloch's kitchen window. The lights were turned off and they had binoculars trained on their own house. Their car was parked in a cul-de-sac half a mile away.

'My arms are getting sore,' Joy complained, resting the binoculars for a moment on her lap.

'Shall I make us another pot of tea?' Rita's voice floated across to them from the doorway.

'I'll do it,' said Joy. 'I need to stretch my legs for a while.'

'Any sign of action out there?' Rita enquired with relish.

Bill shook his head. 'Not a dicky bird. But it's still early.'

'Do you know,' Rita exclaimed. 'This operation reminds me of the blackout. Our neighbour was forever getting into trouble with the warden for not covering the windows properly. It's amazing what little details stick in your mind from back then.'

As Joy switched on the kettle, an eerie red glow was projected around the otherwise dark room.

'I don't think you really need the binoculars, dear,' Rita said to Joy. 'I expect you'll be able to see them arrive clearly enough. They must need a van to transport the goods.'

'You're probably right,' Bill replied, lowering the lenses from his eyes.

'Although, I simply can't imagine those two nice young men being responsible for breaking into my house,' Rita continued, getting into a rhythm with her chatter.

'It's beginning to look unlikely.' Bill sighed heavily.

They drank their teas. Rita perched herself on a stool and joined them for a while. It provided a pleasant opportunity to discuss the war years; Rita from first-hand experience and Bill and Joy from their parents' stories and anecdotes. An hour or so later, Rita went up to bed.

'Why don't you go and have a lie down on the sofa?' Bill asked his wife. 'We can take it in shifts from here.'

'Are you sure?'

'Of course.'

Joy poured out a glass of water from the tap and retired to the sitting room.

Two hours later, Bill could feel his back becoming stiff. He stood up and massaged his lower spine. He glanced at the digital clock face on the cooker. It was half past one.

Bill thought he heard a noise outside. He

scanned the road and pavement but could make out nothing unusual. The sound was like the distant rumble of a vehicle's engine and abruptly, it stopped. Bill picked up the binoculars and looked again. This time he spotted something. A dark van was parked at the kerb, a hundred yards further up the street. The vehicle must have approached without its lights on. The windscreen was completely obscured. He couldn't make out who was inside.

Suddenly, two figures emerged from the front of the van, both with woollen balaclavas pulled low over their faces. The men moved swiftly and silently towards the Hutchisons' house, slipping down the side passage before Bill could even scramble to his feet.

'Joy!' He rasped loudly, rushing into the sitting room to find his wife waking from a doze.

'What is it?'

'They're here! Those men are breaking into our house!'

The plan had been one thing, but the reality of the situation was more shocking than the couple had anticipated.

Bill reached for the phone, dialling 999. 'I just hope the police get there in time.'

Joy leant forward and took her husband's hand. 'Oh, Bill. So do I.'

*

DS Mortimer was asking the Hutchisons questions in their own living room. They'd left Rita's place after the three of them had watched the police cars arrive and several uniformed constables sweep upon the house. About twenty minutes later, two burly officers emerged, with the intruders clearly subdued and under arrest.

The lady detective was obviously confused. 'If you don't mind me asking, what were you doing at your neighbour's house at half past one in the morning?'

'Well, Mrs McCulloch has been rather nervous since her own house was broken into. Sometimes Joy and I go over to keep her company,' Bill explained.

DS Mortimer didn't seem convinced. 'It was certainly fortuitous that you weren't at home when the burglars struck *and* that you happened to be looking out of the window at the exact moment they attempted to enter your property.'

'Yes, you're right, it *was* fortunate,' Bill replied earnestly.

Joy entered with a tray of drinks and biscuits. 'We like to think that our son had something to do with it,' the woman added, by way of explanation. She lifted the framed photograph of Neil off the mantelpiece and handed it to the DS. 'He was tragically taken away from us when just a wee boy, but Neil has a way of letting us know if we are in peril. He speaks to us, you see?'

The detective sergeant cleared her throat. 'I don't think I've got any more questions for you now, Mr and Mrs Hutchison. I'll leave you both to get some rest. My men have sealed up the back door with a panel. It should keep you secure for the time being. Just make sure you get it seen to in the morning. Thanks for the tea.'

Mortimer got to her feet.

Bill stood up, ready to escort her to the front door. 'If you wouldn't mind, we'd like to be kept informed of your investigation. I had a theory, you see, that one of the men responsible for the burglaries might have a military connection. I'm certain this is a detail that a member of your team could look into?'

Mortimer nodded her head, thinking what a strange couple they were. 'I'll call you with an update in a few days.'

When Bill returned to the living room, he slipped an arm around his wife. 'Do you really think that Neil intervened in some way in what happened here tonight?'

Joy shook her head with an amused smile. 'Of course not. I just thought it might be a rather good way of stopping that detective from asking any more questions.'

'Well done, dear. It certainly seemed to work.'

Chapter 35

Craig O'Connor's father had bought his son a series of driving lessons for his seventeenth birthday. The idea was that once he'd passed his test, the lad could start driving him and Val to the pub.

Mick O'Connor stomped up the stairs and paused outside Craig's door, where the lad was sprawled out on the narrow bed with a pair of giant headphones over his ears. Mick took a step forward and wrenched them off.

'Come on lad, I'm taking you out for a lesson in the van. Your 'L' plates have arrived.'

'Do I have to?'

Mick wrapped his podgy fingers around Craig's arm, lifting the boy off the mattress with ease. 'Yes you sodding well do. When I was your age I couldn't wait to get behind the wheel.'

Craig slipped on his glasses and made himself comfortable in the driver's seat. He spent several minutes adjusting the mirrors and making sure the chair position was correct. Mick was just about to lose his patience with all this pansying around when the boy finally placed the key in the ignition.

Agonisingly slowly, Craig drove the vehicle to the junction at the end of their street.

'Turn left,' his father instructed. They proceeded at a snail's pace in the direction of the River View Estate, where Mick thought it would be quiet enough for Craig to practise some manoeuvres.

Suddenly, the boy seemed to realise where they

were headed. 'I'd rather not go onto the new estate, Dad.'

'Why the hell not? You're a bloody liability on the open road.'

Craig said nothing, allowing the vehicle to take them past the high spec new-builds which flanked both sides of this labyrinth of quiet streets. The lad reluctantly acknowledged that his old man was right. He appeared to be making better progress here, his confidence slowly building as a result of knowing they wouldn't be meeting any speeding traffic coming the other way. The lad even managed to perform an emergency stop.

But as they progressed beyond the wide avenues of empty executive homes and the road took them into a barren wasteland secured by high fencing, Craig started to feel his chest tighten.

Sweat had broken out on the lad's forehead and upper lip. The van lurched violently before Craig brought the vehicle to an abrupt halt. He jumped out of the driver's seat and slammed the door shut behind him, proceeding to retch his guts up onto a pile of rubble at the side of the road.

Mick sat immobile in his seat, folding his arms across his fat belly and sighing heavily. He stared out at the desolate landscape which stretched into the distance. The man was wondering just how on earth he and Val had managed to produce such a total wimp.

*

Sally Irving-Bryant was working on a new case. Fortunately for her, the client had admitted to committing the crime for which he was charged but was hoping for mitigation in the sentencing. This was exactly the kind of thing Sally did best. She knew how to manipulate the court system in her favour.

Grant was due home for dinner that evening so Sally had returned to the house early. She was going to have food delivered but wanted to take a shower and get changed before her husband arrived.

The exterior light flickered on as Sally climbed the steps of their Edinburgh townhouse. She stood still for a few moments whilst retrieving the keys from her handbag. Once the door was open, the lawyer felt a weight shove her forward. Before she could work out what was happening, the door was shut behind her and a hand was clamped firmly over her mouth.

'Is there anyone else in the house?' A voice rasped in her ear.

She shook her head, recognising who it was and feeling bile rise into her throat, praying she wasn't going to be sick.

'Don't say a word, okay? I'm only here for information.'

Sally nodded.

Eric Fisher removed his hand and guided her roughly along the corridor to an impressive kitchen. Sally sat down with a thud on one of the dining chairs.

'What do you want?' She demanded, trying to sound brave.

Fisher was pacing up and down beside the worktop which housed a block of Japanese kitchen knives. The sight made her heart race inside her chest.

'I'm living in a poky wee flat on the Southside. I've got no job and I can't go home. Peggy's family want nothing to do with me.' He stopped abruptly and swung round, planting both hands on the side of the thick oak table, as if he was about to tip the whole thing over. 'I want to find the man who butchered my family. This business isn't over, even if the Fiscal thinks it is. That woman who came to visit me in Saughton – she actually seemed to know what she was doing. I want her name and address. She's going to find the bastard for me.'

Sally's breathing had become rapid and shallow. 'I can't possibly give you that information,' she replied weakly.

Eric noticed the lawyer's eyes darting nervously towards the knife block. '*Ah*,' he said gleefully. 'You still believe I'm guilty of knifing my own family. Then you really won't like it if I do this.' The man shot his arm across the worktop and pulled out a long, glistening blade. He immediately held it against Sally's throat. The metal was so sharp that even without any pressure being applied, it was still drawing blood. 'Now, Ms Irving-Bryant. You're going to tell me absolutely everything I want to know and you're going to do it *right now.*'

Chapter 36

When Dani returned from work, she found a man sitting on her doorstep.

'James? What are you doing here?'

James Irving stood up, moving towards the DCI and placing a kiss on her cheek. 'Sally sent me. It's complicated. Can I come in?'

Dani glanced down and noticed a large soft bag by her friend's feet. 'Of course you can.'

James lifted it up and followed her inside.

Bevan left her guest in the kitchen while she got changed and freshened up. When she returned, James had poured them both out a glass of red wine. 'I hope you don't mind. I found an open bottle.'

'Not at all.' Dani took the glass gratefully and sat down. 'Now you can tell me what's going on.'

James sheepishly explained the visit Sally had received from Eric Fisher and how he'd forced her to give him Dani's details. 'She's desperately sorry, especially after everything you've done to help her. But Sal was genuinely terrified. She thought he was going to kill her.'

'I doubt he was but I completely understand. I'm a police officer. It's my job to put myself in harm's way. Sally is a civilian. She shouldn't have hesitated to tell the man what she knew. Fisher would have found out one way or another.'

'Well, Mum and Sally commanded me to come straight here and watch over you.' His cheeks turned pink. 'If you don't mind, that is.'

Dani started to chuckle. 'I am a detective chief

inspector. It's my job to protect other people.'

'But there's no harm in having a little back-up, is there?' James looked put-out.

Dani leant across and took his hand. 'No, there isn't. Any police officer who tries to go it alone is a fool. I really appreciate you coming here. It's actually nice to know that someone cares.'

James' face adopted a serious expression. 'I do care about you Dani. I hope you're aware of that.'

She nodded. 'Yes, James. I am.'

*

Dani called Andy and asked him to come to the flat first thing in the morning. He arrived at 8.30, with a bag of pastries in his hand.

'Morning Ma'am,' he said breezily, sweeping past his boss and heading inside. He stopped abruptly when he spotted James Irving, dressed in casual slacks and a short-sleeved checked shirt. 'Oh, hi.'

'Hello, DC Calder, it's good to see you again.' James put out his hand, which Andy shook reluctantly.

Dani emptied the pastries into a bowl and placed a large pot of coffee on the table. 'Now, if we can put our class differences aside for a moment, we may be able to work as a team on this.'

Andy shot his boss a dirty look, not quite sure what she was insinuating with that comment.

Dani rested her hand on his shoulder and smiled broadly. 'James brought me some important information last night. I think if we put our heads together, we may be able to start piecing out this puzzle.'

Irving helped himself to a croissant, filling Andy in on Eric Fisher's intimidation of his sister.

'So we might be expecting a visit from the scum-bag at any moment,' he replied.

'Hence my decision to meet here. I don't want to miss our friend if does decide to call by.'

Andy reached into his jacket pocket for a notebook and dropped it on the table, flicking ahead to a clean page. He began jotting down notes. 'Can we assume from this, just for the sake of argument, that Eric Fisher is actually innocent of murdering his family.'

Dani nodded. 'But we keep an open mind.'

'And because of Bill and Joy's handiwork in Falkirk, we know that the burglaries on their estate were carried out by Oliver and Dean Sanderson, who used their carpet-cleaning business as a front to find out when the properties would be empty and then did them over. Neither man had any violent convictions. We're assuming that these crimes are unrelated to the murders of the Fishers, the Macallans and Morna Murphy.'

'I spoke to Bill yesterday. He told me that Oliver Sanderson retired from the army a couple of years ago. He was diagnosed as suffering from PTSD after witnessing an IUD explosion in Kandahar. Bill thinks that's why the pair never damaged the photograph of Rita McCulloch's grandson. Sanderson may even have known Christopher.'

James finished off his pastry, taking a sip of coffee to wash it down. 'Dani filled me in on some of the details last night.'

Andy shot him a suspicious look.

'Before she made up the *sofa* for me to sleep on,' he added for clarity. 'Do you really think that these murders are the work of a serial killer?'

Dani took up the mantle. 'We don't get that many pre-meditated murders in Scotland, not outside of the big cities, anyway. There are enough points of similarity to make me think there's one killer.

However, when it comes down to motive, I'm absolutely clueless. Morna Murphy's murder gives the appearance of being sexually motivated, yet there was no sexual assault on the body and there were no wounds to the genitals or breasts as one would expect. Morna had lovers and was physically attractive, like Peggy Fisher, who we also know to have had an affair. This fact could have made them a target for the killer. But the Macallans don't fit this pattern at all. When we take out the theft of the cash box, it's difficult to see who would want that harmless couple dead.'

James considered this for a moment. 'Is there anything that connects these people at all? Have they ever come into contact with one another in the past?'

Dani nodded, admiring the solicitor's logic. 'I've got Phil looking into it. The only possible link we have so far was something Diane Beattie suggested. All of the families had been featured in the local press for some reason or another in the months before the murders. Callum Fisher and the Wheelans because of the lad's footballing achievements, the Murphys because of Lyle's high profile role on the council and Phil has informed me that Nancy Macallan was in the Bankfoot Chronicle with her class two weeks ago, after winning a 'Scotland in Bloom' trophy for the school garden.'

'All of which has brought them to the attention of our killer,' Andy concluded.

'So Peggy's lover, Mark Bannerman, who disappeared just after she and her kids were killed, is *he* your prime suspect for the other murders too?' James glanced from one detective to the other.

'I think he's got to be,' Calder declared, 'especially if Fisher is still clinging to his claim that an intruder butchered the family.'

The lawyer leaned back in his chair. 'Then we need to somehow second guess the guy.'

'How do you mean?' Dani asked.

'These killings are becoming more frequent,' he explained. 'The man is bound to strike again. We need to work out who his next victims are going to be and try to get to them first.'

'How are we going to do that?'

'Have you got a bigger sheet of paper?' Andy enquired.

'I think I've got a sketch pad of Dad's in the bedroom, hold on, I'll have a look.' Dani left the room, returning a few minutes later with a large pad. She ripped off a clean sheet. Andy cleared away the plates and cups so Dani could place it down on the table. Calder leant over it with his pen poised.

'Okay, our first victims were the Fishers; Peggy, Callum, Skye and Kyla. They'd spent their whole lives living in Dalkeith. Next, we have Morna Murphy. She was a similar age to Peggy. Again, she'd lived all her life in Dundee. Then, there's the Macallans; Kenneth and Nancy. They were older than our previous victims, but again, had their roots in Bankfoot. All the targets were local to the east coast of Scotland. We're talking about well-established Scottish families.'

Dani looked carefully at the spider diagram Andy had created on the page. 'You'd better add Peggy's maiden name to the information we've got on the Fishers. It was Wheelan. Mark Bannerman first made contact with Peggy through her parents. He and his father were building their extension.'

Andy added Pat and Rob Wheelan to his diagram. The three stared closely at the information they'd collated.

'We're looking for some kind of pattern, yes?' James said. 'It could be geographic, or to do with education or profession.'

They gazed intently at the words for a good ten minutes.

'I'm just not seeing it,' Dani muttered, her voice filled with exasperation.

'Unless it's the name thing,' Andy Calder said flatly.

'What do you mean?' Dani turned to face her colleague. 'What's significant about the names?'

'Well, it's like what we were discussing the other day, when your dad was moaning about Bryant Construction destroying the Macfie Cairn on Colonsay.'

Dani was puzzled. She had no idea what Calder was driving at.

'The major clans, like the Macfies and the Campbells, they all had subsidiary families - those folk who were always loyal to that particular clan. The names on this list are *all* clan names. In fact, it's more than that, they're all subsidiaries of two particular clans, although they were closely associated with one another. These people are all connected to either the Macdonalds or the MacGregors.'

Chapter 37

Dani stared at the detective constable with a mixture of both awe and scepticism. 'How on earth do you know that?'

'I told you before. It was the only topic I was interested in at school. At one point, I'd memorised every clan name in Scotland and knew who they'd been loyal to before the Union. I used to give the kids at school with pro-English surnames a hard time in the playground. Nothing serious, just a wee shove in the dinner queue once in a while. They had absolutely no idea why I was doing it.'

James took a step forward. 'Alright, it's a connection of sorts, but where does it take us?'

'I think we should sit back down and have a wee history lesson. Andy, tell us everything you know about the Macdonalds and the MacGregors.'

They pulled up their chairs and listened, whilst Calder entertained them with tales of Jacobite uprisings and religious divisions. 'Probably the most famous story relating to the Macdonalds is the Glencoe Massacre.'

'I've actually heard of that,' Dani chipped in for good measure.

'In 1692, the staunchly protestant William and Mary were on the English throne, yet the majority of the Scottish Highlanders remained Catholic. They were sympathetic to James VII, who was in exile in France. William and Mary, fearing a rebellion north of the border, insisted that an oath of allegiance be sworn to them. Alexander Macdonald of Glencoe made it a point of honour to delay taking the oath until the very last moment. Due to a mix-up, he didn't actually swear allegiance until a week after the deadline. So the English Secretary of State decided to make an example of him. Letters of fire and sword were issued against the Macdonalds, with an eye to dispersing the clan entirely, as had been done to the MacGregors a century earlier.

This bloody task was given to the troops of Campbell of Glenlyon. The Campbells had enjoyed the hospitality of the Macdonalds for two weeks. Then, on the night of the 12th-13th February, they murdered forty of their hosts, in cold blood. But many of the Macdonalds managed to escape. The clan was not successfully broken up, as the English had hoped. In fact, the atrocity intensified anti-English feeling, even in the Lowlands.'

'So all those people were massacred and it was for nothing in the end?' James said.

'Aye, that's pretty much the case. As you can see from this list, there are still plenty of Macdonalds left in Scotland. The Campbells never succeeded in wiping them all out.'

'What if someone's trying to finish the job now?' Dani said quietly.

'Some ghostly member of the clan Campbell, you mean - back from the dead, sporting a kilt and sporran and wielding his claymore?' James chuckled at the vision that had formed in his head.

'Not a *ghost* James, a real, living and breathing man. Somebody who believes that he's ridding Scotland of a disloyal element – a person who feels as if the Union itself is in danger.'

'The Union *is* in bloody danger,' Andy Calder snorted. 'We very nearly left it and we still might.'

'*Exactly*,' Dani replied. 'We've been living through turbulent times. Whichever side of the fence you happened to be on, we cannot deny that the referendum caused divisions; between husbands and wives, sons and daughters.' As she glanced at the men opposite her, Dani could imagine quite clearly which side both had been on. As for herself, Dani's Welsh heritage had made it very difficult to come to a decision.

'Well, I suppose it is a motive,' James conceded. 'So how do we try and work out who might be next? There must be hundreds of Macdonalds in Scotland.'

'There are other patterns here too,' Dani stated decisively. 'We're only looking at eastern Scotland for starters. We have to assume that our killer lives somewhere within this radius. In fact, we've got a computer system at headquarters that could give us a good idea of where the perpetrator is based, if we enter the locations of the murders into the programme.'

'We've hardly ever used it,' Andy put in.

'That's because serial murders are so rare in Scotland,' his boss replied. 'I can ask Phil to run the data today.'

'Is it safe to assume that our guy is keeping an eye on local media to select his next victims? If he spots someone with the right name, they become his target.'

'Then we need to do the same.' Dani felt the coffee pot and discovered it was stone cold.

'That's going to be a huge task.' Andy sighed heavily. 'We really need another piece of evidence to narrow the search.'

They didn't have a chance to discuss this possibility any further. All three heard a noise outside. It sounded like a milk bottle being kicked over. Dani got to her feet. 'Andy, if you go round the back, I'll check the front.'

'Sure thing, Ma'am.'

'What can I do?' James asked.

'Make some more coffee,' Dani called over her shoulder, as she jogged down the hallway to the front door.

Dani opened it gingerly and scanned the path. There was nothing. She stepped outside and kept close to the wall of the house, following it round to the left, where a passage ran along the side of the property. As she turned her head to look down the alleyway, Dani saw a tall figure, dressed in dark clothing, pressed up against the brickwork beside the kitchen window. The DCI moved forward and stood firm at the entrance, shouting into the gloom, 'Eric, I know you're here to see me. I'm prepared to talk to you. There's no need for this 'cloak and dagger' act.'

The man abruptly turned. As he did so, Andy leapt out of the bushes and grappled him into an arm lock. 'Drop it!' Calder commanded.

Dani could see then that Fisher had a long sliver of broken glass in his hand, which immediately fell to the stony ground. She strode down to join her colleague.

Eric turned his face towards her. 'DCI Bevan. I need to talk to you urgently. I don't mean anyone any harm.'

'Then what's with the weapon?'

'Self-defence, Detective. If you'd spent a year in Saughton as a child-killer, you'd know what I meant by that.' The man eyed her defiantly.

'Bring him inside,' she instructed Calder.

James had done what he was told and made a fresh pot of coffee. Tactfully, he had removed their notes on the Fisher case and tidied them away out of sight.

Calder led Eric to the table and indicated he should sit down. Dani poured him a coffee, which he gulped at greedily.

Irving puffed himself up and stood before the man. 'My sister has a nasty gash across her throat. She truly thought you were going to kill her.'

Eric looked up. 'I'm sorry about that. But Ms Irving-Bryant believes I murdered my family. I wasn't going to get anything out of her unless I played up to her expectations of me. I hope it doesn't leave a scar.' He absent-mindedly touched the damaged flesh around his own neck.

James shuffled off and found a seat, knowing he would have to be satisfied with that.

When Fisher had finished his drink, he turned to address Dani. 'When you came to visit me in prison, it gave me hope. You were the first person who'd even entertained the idea I might be innocent. I've lost my wife and kids. My freedom isn't worth anything to me. All I want is to track down the bastard who did this. Can you help?'

'I believe you. I think there was somebody else in your house that afternoon. I also think he's killed others, too.' Dani took a deep breath. 'Did you know your wife was having a relationship with another man?'

Eric bristled. 'Yes, I did.'

'You realise it gives you a motive to kill Peggy?'

Anger flashed across his unshaven face. 'I loved Peggy. It was over with this other guy, we'd worked stuff out. But even if we hadn't, why the hell would I kill my kids? They were all I ever really had.' The man suddenly crumpled, his body juddering with sobs. Dani suspected that he'd been keeping in his grief for a very long time. She laid a hand on his back. 'When I found out about her and Bannerman, I made Peggy organise a paternity test for me and the twins. After I knew I really was their dad, we decided to try again to make the marriage work.'

'So had Peggy told Bannerman it was over?'

Eric nodded, his face buried in his hands. 'She must have done.'

Dani pulled out a chair and sat down to face Fisher. 'Do you think it was Bannerman who bundled you into the cupboard and then dragged you down those stairs?'

Eric shook his head. 'I'd only seen the guy once, from a distance. I just don't know.'

'But the man's been missing since it happened, it's got to have been him,' Calder insisted.

Eric wiped his eyes and addressed the room. 'Yeah, it's possible. But this guy could have changed his name umpteen times since then and taken on new jobs, new identities. All I can tell you is that the bloke who was in my house was *big*. He was strong and relentless, like he was on some kind of mission.'

Dani leant forward. 'If you want us to find this man then you'll need to leave us to it. I want you to return to your flat in Edinburgh and stay there. I promise to keep you updated on what we discover but you'll have to trust me and not interfere.'

Eric directed his gaze towards the DCI, slowly nodding his agreement.

Chapter 38

The school hall was full of trestle tables. Each one packed with homemade items for sale. Louise Keene's table contained an impressive display of cakes and preserves, which she'd carefully wrapped and finished off with pretty, colourful ribbons.

On the stall next to hers, Louise's friend Laura had set out various hand-knitted baby clothes and booties. The woman was fussing around her merchandise, trying to position the items as attractively as possible. 'Your stall looks so professional, Lou. How on earth did you manage it – with the boys running around your feet?'

'I did the baking while they were at school.' Louise omitted to mention the fact that Davy had helped her to decorate the jars and boxes. She just smiled happily instead, as the memory sent a warm sensation tingling through her body.

Laura tilted her head to one side and examined her friend closely. 'There's something different about you.' She waggled her finger. 'Have you been going to Weightwatchers at the Town Hall? We said we'd do it together!'

Louise laughed. 'I haven't, I promise. I'm just bloody relieved that this building work's finished. The boys have got so much more space now. It really makes a difference.'

Her friend still looked suspicious. 'Have things calmed down for Fergus at work?'

Louise shrugged. 'It's better than it was. He's promised to take me out to dinner at the weekend.'

Laura noted that the woman didn't appear particularly enthusiastic about the prospect. But before she could interrogate her friend any further, a man with a large camera around his neck approached them.

'Afternoon ladies, I'm from the Glenrothes Gazette,' He boomed, eyeing Louise's stall with obvious admiration. 'I think you're going to make a great deal of money for charity today.'

He directed Louise to stand squarely behind her produce, stretching out her arms to encompass the display. 'Gorgeous!' He declared, snapping away feverishly. 'I believe we've got ourselves a lovely front-page. I'll just need to take a note of your names for the caption.'

*

Ben was the last one to settle. Louise sat on the edge of his bed and ruffled his thick, dark hair. 'How early can I get up in the morning, Mum?' He asked sleepily.

Louise picked up the bedside clock, which had a glowing face doubling as a night light. 'When this little hand is on the seven and the long hand is on the twelve you can get up. But stay in your room please. Don't wake your brother if he's still asleep.'

'Okay.'

She kissed him on the forehead, watching her eldest son's eyelids flicker as he drifted off into blissful oblivion.

Louise checked on Jamie and then padded down the stairs. Fergus had promised he'd be home for dinner. She turned the oven off and began laying the table in the kitchen, something they didn't normally do on a weeknight. For the first time since she'd started having a relationship with Davy, Louise felt guilty. She supposed it was amazing to not have felt that way before. But the first few encounters she'd had with her lover were so euphoric that it was hard to imagine what they were doing was wrong. Louise hadn't experienced such a sense of joy since she was a little girl, before Neil had died. It seemed incredibly cruel that anyone would want to deny her that feeling.

Louise lifted the fish pie out onto the worktop and shook some frozen peas into a saucepan. She'd just poured water on top and set them over a light when the front door opened.

Fergus Keene laid his jacket down on the sofa and deposited his briefcase on the floor. Hearing noises in the kitchen, he walked through to find his wife preparing dinner. Fergus kissed her on the cheek.

'Are the boys asleep?'

She nodded. 'Don't go upstairs for ten minutes, you might wake them.'

'Okay.' Fergus slid a bottle of wine out of the rack and began opening it. 'This looks nice, is there a special occasion?'

'No, I just thought it might be good to talk.'

Louise dished up the food whilst her husband used the downstairs toilet to have a wash.

They sat down opposite one another a little awkwardly. Fergus had been working such long hours recently that they'd hardly had a proper conversation in months, let alone touched each other or made love.

'The charity fayre went well today. I nearly sold out of cakes. The boys ate the last few at teatime.'

He smiled. 'Great. You worked really hard to prepare, I'm glad it paid off. Did the lads behave themselves?'

'Well, you know, the usual.' Louise took a

mouthful of pie, but it seemed strangely tasteless. 'A man from the Gazette was there. He took a photograph of Laura and me. He said we might be on the front page.'

'Terrific. We'll have to get an extra copy to send to your parents, they'll absolutely love that.'

'The thing is, when he asked for my name, I told him it was Louise Hutchison, not Keene. I don't know why I said it. We've been married ten years for heaven's sake. I suppose I was just flustered and it was the first name that came into my head.'

'It doesn't matter, love. It *was* your surname for a long time.' He took a sip of wine and beamed. 'Don't worry, I forgive you.'

Quite unexpectedly, tears began to stream down Louise's cheeks. Fergus let his cutlery clatter onto the plate, standing up and moving over to place his arms around his wife. 'Darling, what on earth is the matter?'

She buried her face into his chest and sobbed. 'I've missed you that's all. I've just missed you.'

Chapter 39

After Eric Fisher had gone, James brought the rolled up sheet of paper they'd been working on down from a shelf. 'Do you believe the man will do as he's told?' He asked Dani.

'Probably not, but I sincerely hope he does. I'll have to be careful what I tell him, I've got a feeling that Eric isn't intending to bring the murderer of his family to trial.'

'You think that if Fisher finds this guy first, he'll kill him?'

'I'm certain of it,' added Calder. 'Eric Fisher is a man with absolutely nothing to lose.'

The phone started ringing in the hallway. Dani went out to answer it. 'Oh, hi Dad. How's things?' She carried the receiver back into the kitchen to re-join the others. 'That's great news. I don't think it had anything to do with me at all. Listen, Dad, what do you know about the clan Macdonald? I know it's an odd question, just humour me.' Dani perched on a seat whilst she absorbed her father's words. Bevan had always found him to be a mine of information. She supposed it came with the job. 'Great,' she said finally. 'I'll keep you posted on what's happening at this end. Take care, bye.' Dani ended the call.

'What did he have to say?' Andy asked casually.

'Bryant Construction have agreed to work around the Macfie cairn, in return for some favourable publicity in the local newspaper.'

'Just warn your dad not to get himself on the front page.' Andy chuckled.

Dani shot him a worried glance.

'Don't worry, Ma'am, it was only a joke. The last time I checked, the name Bevan didn't have a lot to do with Scottish clansmen.'

'I'm glad Grant was reasonable about the situation,' said James, ignoring this exchange. 'He can be a tough businessman. It's hard to change his mind about something, as Sally has learnt to her cost on occasion.'

'My dad can be strangely persuasive,' Dani added.

'What did he say about the Macdonalds? I can't claim to be a world expert on the subject,' Andy put-in.

'Dad said that the history of the clans in Scotland is one of loyalties. The Macdonalds and the McGregors were determined to maintain the Celtic way of life, fiercely protecting it from invaders. The Normans, the English and even the Vikings have tried at various times to overpower Scotland and bring it to heel. But after the Union of 1707, Dad says that the story began to change. Following the Great Civil War in the middle of the 18th Century, the Celtic way of life gradually died out, more Scots became loyal to the English ruling classes. This was seen most notably within the military. The Highland Regiments, made up of clans like the Campbells and the Mackays, helped to impose the British social system on the Highlands.'

'So would folk in the Scottish military be more likely to be loyal to the Union?' James asked, thinking guiltily that at the private school he'd attended in Edinburgh, they had only learnt about English History.

'On the whole, yes. But particularly so if they were members of ancient regiments like the Black Watch, who fought in the service of the British

Empire for over two hundred years.'

Andy scratched his head. 'We're coming back to this military connection again. Bill Hutchison thought it was important.'

'That was in the case of the burglaries in Falkirk, not our murders,' Dani pointed out.

'I realise that, but haven't we learnt by now to take Hutchison's instincts seriously? Maybe we should be looking for a man who's serving in the army. He may feel as if everything he has done in his career has been for nothing, if there are people in Scotland working to bring the Union to an end. He may have convinced himself that he's some kind of clan warrior.'

James nodded his head. 'Actually, that makes sense. It would also help to explain how well this person has covered their tracks. If he's a trained killer, it could make sense.'

'Yes, it could.' Dani fell silent.

James sighed, scanning through the details written on the page laid out before them. 'It just feels as if this person can't quite be human. The way he slips in and out of the houses without leaving a trace. I can almost picture him being that ghostly Highland Chieftain, disappearing into the mists after he's destroyed his prey.'

'Oh, he's flesh and blood all right, James. Be in no doubt about that. Sadly, they always are.'

*

When Dani had seen Calder out of the door, she returned to her guest. He stood up and moved towards the DCI, pausing before they were actually touching.

'Do you want me to leave as well? I suppose you aren't really in danger from Fisher any longer.'

Dani took a step nearer, stretching up on her toes to place a kiss on his lips. James wrapped his arms around her and pulled Dani close.

'I don't want you to leave, no.'

'Good,' he muttered quietly, finding her lips again with his own and gently manoeuvring her backwards towards the bedroom.

Dani suddenly placed her hand on his chest, to halt their progress. 'I've been here before James. Somehow, I always end up getting hurt.'

He clasped Dani's hand, lowering it back down to rest by her side. 'Not this time.' Unexpectedly, he lifted her up, carrying her gingerly the rest of the way. 'You know you can trust me, DCI Bevan. I'm a lawyer.'

Dani laughed heartily at this, until James had managed to get her inside and kick the door shut behind them.

Chapter 40

Eric Fisher hadn't bothered to do much with the flat. His old house in Dalkeith had been given a lick of paint by a mate of his and was currently being rented out to a couple from Latvia. The council didn't know anything about it, but that was the least of his worries. Fisher couldn't quite believe that anyone would want to live in the place after what had happened there, but his mate said the tenants were lining up. There was no accounting for some folk.

The room he was sitting in had a bay window. Because the flat was on the top floor, he could just make out the Pentland Hills in the distance, over the grey rooftops of Auld Reekie. Eric walked across to the window and pulled aside the grubby net curtain, which was making the place feel gloomy. There was no need for the thing at all, the flat was hardly overlooked.

There was a small kitchenette leading off the living room, which also possessed a small window in the eaves. Eric wandered in there to prepare a cup of tea. He was exhausted after his trip to Glasgow. It had taken all his energy, emotional and physical. Fisher intended simply to exist now, until he received news from DCI Bevan, then he could set in motion his plan to obliterate the man who killed his family. But he would need all his strength in order to complete the task. With this in mind, Eric reached into a cupboard for a tin of corned beef. He rolled back the pin, thinking how arcane this process was, like something from the 1950s.

As he flipped back the lid on the bread bin and lifted out a sliced loaf, Eric thought he saw something pass by the little window. He immediately leaned forward, his hands resting on the sink and peered out. There was nothing to see except the lead tiles on the roof. Eric imagined it must have been a pigeon. Some of those birds were so fat they could easily pass for a small animal. He recalled how he'd had to tell Callum off for chasing them once, when they'd taken him on a trip to the Castle as a wee boy.

Eric had to grip the worktop tightly, until the surge of anger that this memory had triggered began to recede. He buttered the bread thickly and added some slabs of the processed beef, taking the sandwich and his mug of tea back into the lounge. He sat on the battered leather sofa to eat it.

As soon as his belly was full, he leant back against the cushions and closed his eyes. When he awoke, the flat was in darkness. The empty plate was still resting on his lap. The mug had tipped over onto its side, a trickle of beige liquid dribbling out onto the sofa cushion.

'Shit,' he muttered under his breath. Eric took the crockery into the kitchen, returning with a damp cloth. He leant over and wiped up the mess, glad that the sofa wasn't upholstered. Suddenly, his body flinched. He'd sensed that movement again. It wasn't outside the window this time, but inside the flat.

Eric knew he must remain perfectly still. He swivelled his eyes back and forth, to see what could be discerned in his peripheral vision. The man froze. He could make out a dark shadow in the corner of the room. It was tall and wide. Eric tried to calculate whether he'd be able to reach the front door before the shadow reached him. He didn't much rate his chances.

The shadow shifted. Eric turned and bolted towards the hallway. Halfway along, he was barged into the wall. His face took the brunt of the impact and Fisher could identify the metallic taste of blood in his mouth. He'd probably cut his lip.

Eric was a big man. He tried to shake his assailant off, but the weight pressing down on him was too great. Knowing that he was not at an advantage, Eric decided to go down fighting. He sent his foot flying backwards sharply, catching the man on the shins. 'Bastard!' He hissed, as the figure behind him loosened his grip for just a second.

Fisher summoned up all his strength and shot out an elbow, hoping he'd caught the guy in the ribs. But all Eric had succeeded in doing was riling up his nemesis even further. Within seconds, his arms were pulled up painfully high behind his back and his body was pushed flat against the paintwork.

There was a momentary pause and then Eric felt the knife go in. It seemed to slice straight through his esophagus. Fisher braced himself for more blows. Then he realised there would be none. The blade was so long that it had passed straight through his neck and penetrated the soft plasterboard beyond, pinning him to its surface like a butterfly placed on display in a museum.

He knew then that this was how he was to go - trapped here until the lifeblood had finally drained out of his body.

The monster had not even permitted him the mercy of a quick death.

Chapter 41

Dci Annie Carmichael pulled aside the plastic curtain which was obscuring the murder scene.

Dani gasped. 'Good God.' She took a tentative step closer.

'Don't get too near. The floor is awash with his blood.'

'When are you going to bring him down?'

'The pathologist hasn't arrived yet, if you can believe it. Our techs have taken plenty of photos. As soon as she's done her job, we can get him bagged up and off to the mortuary. It looks as if the murderer got in through a window in the bedroom. There's fairly easy access across the rooftops, as long as you don't suffer from vertigo, of course. The attacker could have climbed up any of the external fire escapes. It wasn't difficult.'

'Would Eric have known much about it?' Dani tried her best not to allow her eyes to drift back towards the limp shell that was once Eric Fisher.

'It looks as if Fisher was trying to make a run for the door. The attacker shoved him against the wall, here. I'm afraid that Eric would have been alive for a certain amount of time after the blade went in. I'll have to wait for the pathologist to confirm it absolutely, but I've seen enough to be pretty sure the man bled to death.'

'Shit. He was at my place only a couple of days ago. Fisher wanted my help to track down the person who killed his family.'

'It looks as if he tracked down Eric first.'

Dani shook her head in frustration. 'I should have seen this coming.'

'You mean *I* should,' Carmichael said stonily. 'If I'd taken Fisher's version of events seriously, then I would have been treating Eric Fisher as a witness to a bloody multiple murder. It was *my* job to protect him. Christ, the guy was better off when he was in Saughton.' She ran a hand through her sculpted hair.

'It isn't your fault, Annie. I don't believe that was why Eric was killed.' Dani explained their theory about the murderer targeting those connected to the Macdonald clan, perfectly aware of how off-the-wall it sounded.

'To be honest, Dani, I'm willing to entertain anything. If you want to bring your DC over, I'll give you both a desk. I'll even lend you the use of DC Webber. The two of you seemed to get on pretty well last time. I'll even set aside some money from my budget to put you up at a hotel. Hell, I'll bake you a bloody cake if you can solve this one for me.'

Dani chuckled. 'I'll speak with DCS Nicholson. He won't be happy about the bad publicity that having a serial killer on the loose will generate. I'm certain he'll agree.'

'Great, just show up at headquarters whenever you're ready.'

'Thanks. Oh and Annie, I'll only need a hotel room for my detective constable. I've got a friend who lives in the city. I can stay with him.'

Annie put her hands up in the air. 'You can bunk up with whoever you like, my dear. Just help me find this monster, before the bastard strikes again.'

*

DC Alec Webber looked pleased to see the Glasgow detectives. He'd cleared a place for them at his workstation. 'I'm really glad to have your help,' the younger man declared. 'Because I've been drawing a total blank in the search for Mark Bannerman. I'm fairly certain he didn't leave the country. It's really not that easy to get hold of a false passport. Bannerman hadn't ever been issued with one, his mother confirmed this. He'd never been out of Britain before he disappeared.'

'Might he have taken on a different name?' Andy Calder asked.

'Yes, I think he probably did, but I've not been able to find out what identity he's living under. The boss did an appeal on Crime Scotland last week. We got a few hundred responses to the photographs that were shown, but none of them panned out. The guy's vanished into thin air.'

'Then maybe we can pursue this other line of inquiry - focussing on the victims rather than the perpetrator.' Dani laid out the results of the offender proximity programme that Phil ran for them back at Pitt Street. 'When we added the locations of the murders, the computer threw up a circular area, roughly ten miles in diameter, that sits about here,' she pointed to a circle marked out in red.

'It's approximately halfway between Stirling and Crieff. That feels like a long distance from Dalkeith,' Alec remarked.

Dani nodded. 'It is, but we've got murder sites as far north as Bankfoot and Dundee. This widens out the parameters.'

'So, as far as major residential areas go, there's Dunblane and Auchterarder. Then it's the towns and villages in between. So our guy could be living in any one of these places,' Andy stated.

Dani perched on the edge of the desk. 'We have this theory that our man could be in the military. Are there any army bases within close proximity?'

The DCI eyed her two colleagues.

Webber shrugged his shoulders. 'I'm not sure, Ma'am, but I could check it out?'

'Yes please, Alec. I believe that we're looking for someone who's had a rough ride during their military career. Maybe they've suffered from psychological problems due to their time in the field. This may have triggered the man's homicidal delusions.'

DCI Carmichael approached them from her office. 'The PM results are back on Fisher.'

Dani raised her eyebrows expectantly.

'He died sometime between 9pm and midnight on Saturday. The pathologist reckons it took 45 minutes for the guy to bleed out. Hopefully, at some stage Eric lost consciousness. But he was a big, healthy bloke. I think he was probably awake for most of it.'

'Bloody hell,' Andy muttered.

'None of the neighbours saw or heard a damn thing. The two flats on either side of Fisher's were empty. It's like everything's operating in our man's favour.'

'Then we'll see if we can't turn the tables on him,' Dani declared.

'There's something else,' Carmichael went on. 'One of the techies found a letter in a box under Fisher's bed. It was tied up along with photographs of Peggy and the kids. It's addressed to Sally Irving Bryant.'

'Have you read it yet?'

'I thought I'd leave that to you.'

Carmichael fished the envelope out of her pocket and handed it to Dani.

Bevan took it gingerly, as if it might somehow be radioactive. She glanced at her fellow officers before carefully slicing it open.

HMP Edinburgh
Wing 17
April, 2015

Ms Irving-Bryant,

I know you don't believe I'm innocent. I'm not an idiot and can see the way you look at me, as if you think I'm about to reach forward and cut your throat. I wish you'd had faith in me without my having to provide this information. But I suppose that was too much to hope for.

I expect I'll spend the rest of my life behind bars, because the bastard who did this was just too clever in the end - cleverer that you realise, Ms Irving Bryant. He made it so that I couldn't tell you the whole story, out of shame and disgust. But if I'm found guilty at the trial, I will hand you this letter as I go down. Then at least someone will know the truth of what happened.

I'm not a saint and I've done things I'm not proud of, but I'd never hurt my wife and kids, that's different.

I told you that I was locked in the cupboard for the whole time my family was being attacked. That wasn't entirely true. After ten minutes or so, he brought me out. The scum-bag put the hood over my head and a knife to my throat, just like I said. But before he dragged me down to the kitchen, he made me do something. This is the hardest thing I've ever had to admit to.

He shoved a knife in my hand and told me to stab hard with it. At first, I shook my head, so he dug the blade deep into my skin, so that it pierced the surface and drew blood. So I did what he said. The knife that I was holding penetrated soft flesh and I heard a whimper.

He'd made me put the blade into Callum. Then he shoved me down the stairs and forced me to do the same thing again. Just one thrust. I don't think Peggy was aware of what was going on. She was unconscious, or long gone by this point. I hope it was the last.

Then I was on the kitchen floor. The rest happened exactly as I said. He made me swallow the pills and afterwards he slit my throat.

You might ask why I did the awful things he forced me to, when I believed he was going to kill me anyway. The only answer I can provide is that you don't know how you're going to react when someone is threatening your life. I discovered that if there's a knife to your throat then you'll say or do anything to save your skin. You'd betray your own mother and that's the truth.

So that is why I had Callum and Peggy's blood on my clothes, Ms Irving-Bryant. The evidence was pretty damning and the bastard knew it. He's clever, but more than that, he's evil. I know this, because I smelt his sour breath on my face, felt his steady heartbeat and could sense he had no mercy.

You can do what you like with this letter. I've only written it because that woman detective you brought with you today seemed like she might believe me. Maybe you could pass it on to her? I reckon that despite the evidence she could tell I didn't kill them. Some people have got good instincts, haven't they?

My anger is the only thing keeping me alive - I want that monster found. If this letter helps to do it, then I'm glad I've written it.
Yours Sincerely,

Eric Fisher.

Chapter 42

Craig O'Connor had been ill for over a week. Val didn't usually worry about this kind of thing. She tended to leave her children to it when they were poorly. The symptoms always seemed to pass after a few days. But this time it was different.

Ever since Mick had taken him on that poxy driving lesson the boy had been a mess. He didn't have much meat on his bones as it was but the lad was now positively skeletal.

Val stomped up the stairs carrying a tray. On it was a bowl of tomato soup and a buttered roll. She stopped in the doorway, momentarily shocked by the paleness of her son's skin. 'I've brought you some lunch. I want you to try and eat it, son. Otherwise I'll need to bring in the doctor.'

Craig shook his head violently, his greasy hair whipping his pallid cheeks. 'No! I don't need the doctor.'

'Then get this down you,' his mother commanded, slipping the tray onto his lap.

The boy almost gagged at the smell, but allowed Val to slowly spoon the hot liquid into his mouth, dutifully swallowing it down. The woman lowered her voice. 'What happened when you went out in the van, son? Did your dad do something to you? You know you can tell me, I've no illusions about that mean old sod.'

'No, Dad didn't do a thing.' Craig began shaking uncontrollably, beads of sweat springing to his brow.

Val let the spoon clatter into the bowl. 'Then what in hell's name is the matter!' She poked a fat finger into his ribs, suddenly remembering something she'd heard about on the Jeremy Kyle show called 'tough love'. 'You're going to tell me what this is all about Craig O'Connor and you're going to tell me *right now*, otherwise I'll kick you out into that street on your useless bony arse!'

*

This time Dani was driven down the O'Connors' street, it wasn't in Annie Carmichael's swanky BMW. Instead, it was DC Webber who was behind the wheel.

'The woman wasn't very coherent on the phone,' Webber explained, as they got out of the car and approached the front door. 'All I managed to decipher was that her son had something to tell us.'

Val wrenched the door open before they'd even rung the bell. 'About bloody time,' she seethed.

The woman led the police officers into the grubby kitchen. Dani had to suppress a gasp when she caught sight of Craig. He looked as if he was at death's door. She wondered what on earth had happened to the lad.

Val told them to sit down at the table, mumbling that she would make them all tea.

Dani turned her attention towards the young man opposite, who had his head hung low. 'Now, Craig, what's this all about?'

The DCI could hear the boy's shallow breathing. She decided that here was a person eaten up by something – guilt, perhaps?

Val clattered the cups loudly.

Craig shot his head up to meet Dani's gaze. There was a flash of fear in his eyes, but then she got it. The fear was of his mother. Val was the reason why they were here. The boy wouldn't be talking otherwise.

'Well?' Dani prompted, a little more harshly this time, taking Val's lead.

'I didn't tell you everything, when you were last here.' Craig started picking at a scratch on the table, making it considerably larger. 'I don't want Eric to know I've spoken to you.'

'That won't be difficult. He's dead.'

Craig shot backwards in his seat, as if Dani had slapped him in the face. 'What?'

'He was murdered in his flat in Edinburgh on Saturday night. So if you've got something you need to tell us, Craig, I sincerely suggest you do it now. I'd hate to think it might be *you* next.'

'*Who* killed him?' The boy was almost panic-stricken. 'He can't have come back for us - we *buried* him for God's sake. I don't understand!'

'Buried *who*, Craig?' Dani was rapidly losing her patience.

'Bannerman. Peggy's boyfriend.'

Dani shot a glance at Webber. 'I think you need to tell us the whole story,' she said quietly. 'Right from the very beginning.'

Craig took a sip of the mahogany coloured tea his mother had placed before him. 'We'd been working on the houses at the River View Estate for a few weeks. Eric was really enjoying designing the interiors. The development company liked what we were doing and allowed Eric pretty much free rein to choose the materials. One morning, he decided that he wanted a particular type of handle for the kitchen units. You couldn't get them at the wholesalers, only at a shop in town. So we both took the van into Dalkeith. As we walked past one of the cafés, Eric stopped.

He'd seen Peggy inside. She was with some bloke. Eric didn't say anything about it that day, but for the next couple of weeks, every so often, Eric would take the van into town for a couple of hours, leaving me to carry on with the job.

On one occasion, he'd been gone for a long while. I'd done everything I could at the site and was sitting on the step outside waiting for him. Eventually, the van pulled up. Eric looked really flustered. He told me to get in. He drove through the estate and out into the wasteland beyond, we kept going for ages, stopping at a place where the fence had been damaged and there was a small gap in the wire.

It was beginning to get dark by this time. Eric hadn't said much until then, but whilst we were parked up he explained that there'd been an accident. He knew that Peggy had been seeing somebody. For a few weeks he'd been watching them together. That day, he followed the man home in the van. His name was Mark Bannerman. Eric was planning to confront him and tell the guy to steer clear of Peggy, maybe rough the idiot up a bit. But he said that this bloke was full of shit. He claimed he was in love with Peggy and he was going to look after her. Then he made the mistake of telling Eric that he wanted to take on the kids too – *his* kids.

There was nobody at home in this bloke's house and Eric started hitting the guy. He said he couldn't bear to see his smug face telling him he was about to take away his children. When he'd stopped, Bannerman wasn't moving. Eric pulled the van up to the side of the house and put Bannerman in the back.

By the time I saw the body, Eric had wrapped it up in bin-bags. I don't know where he did that, he never told me. Eric needed me to help him bury it. He swore it was an accident, but that if Peggy ever found out it would kill her.

Eric had brought two spades. We dug for hours

and hours, the ground was so hard. Eventually, we felt like it was deep enough. It took the two of us to drag him through the hole in the fence. Bannerman must have been a really big fella. We placed a couple of concrete slabs that we'd found over the top of the grave.'

'Do you think you could show us exactly where he's buried?' Dani asked.

'If no one's fixed the fence yet then I reckon so. There were some electricity pylons nearby too.'

'Okay. We'll need to organise a search team to take us out there, Craig.'

He nodded. 'I didn't kill Bannerman, I swear. When I heard about what happened to Eric's family at the house, I thought that Peggy must have found out somehow about what Eric had done to her boyfriend. I reckoned she'd confronted him and he'd flipped out, killing them all. I thought that with Eric in prison, it was the end of it. Justice had been done.'

'What about Mark Bannerman's family? Surely they had a right to know where their son was.'

Craig gulped down his tea loudly. For the first time since arriving at the house, Dani saw some colour rush to his cheeks. Then a thought struck her.

'Craig. Was the only reason you kept quiet about the body because you were worried it might upset Peggy, or was there something else?'

The lad's eyes darted back and forth.

'What's she talking about?' Val piped up from her position at the sink, sensing there was a piece of information that she'd not already been told.

'We never found the money that Eric Fisher had earned from his work on the new builds at the River View Estate. Mr Fisher claimed he'd spent it all at the pub and on gifts for Callum's birthday. That wasn't true though, was it? Eric gave *you* that money, to keep your mouth shut about helping him to dispose of the body. Were you actually intending to admit to that element of the story, Craig?'

The lad hung his head once again.

Before Bevan or Webber could do anything to stop her, Val had swept across the room and given her son a violent clip around the ear. 'You didn't tell me *that* part, you greedy little bugger!'

Chapter 43

Joy Hutchison slipped the glossy pages out of the envelope and examined them closely. 'Bill, come and take a look. Louise has sent us the prints she had made of Neil's photograph.'

Her husband came into the kitchen to join her. 'Goodness, they've come out really well. I wasn't expecting the quality to be as good as that.' He placed an arm around his wife's waist. 'Are you okay?'

She nodded, smiling. 'Yes, I am. It's just a relief to know that we've got copies.'

'Is there anything else inside?' Bill tipped up the jiffy bag and shook out the rest of the contents, which included a clipping from the Glenrothes Gazette.

Joy picked it up. 'Oh, look. It's the front page feature about Louise's stall at the charity fayre. What a lovely picture.'

Bill beamed proudly. 'I think we should frame this too. Then we can put it alongside Neil's photo on the mantelpiece.'

'Yes, I'd like that.' Joy gave a sigh, resting her head contentedly against her husband's shoulder.

*

The wind was blowing relentlessly across the vast expanse of wasteland to the west of Dalkeith. It hadn't proved so easy for Craig O'Connor to identify the grave site. There were hundreds of metres of fencing and much of it had been damaged by vandals in the months since they buried Mark

Bannerman's body. They were focussing their search to within a half mile of the imposing line of electricity pylons which stretched off towards the A7.

Bevan, Calder and Webber stood by and watched. Their padded jackets zipped up to the neck.

'No wonder I had so much trouble tracing Mark. The guy was dead the whole time.'

'I think we underestimated Eric Fisher. He must have called Bannerman's father, either pretending to be his son or a friend, perhaps. He told Gus that Mark was leaving with a woman he'd met and wouldn't be back. It was clever. Bannerman's parents barely lifted a finger to find their son. We might never have found out either, if Craig hadn't cracked. Eric didn't feel the need to confess to this particular dirty deed.'

'No wonder Eric didn't mention the money to the police. He'd used it to hush up a murder.' Calder added, 'where *was* the money by the way?'

'Under Craig's bed. His mother believes that was why he spent so much time lying on it.' Dani gave a grim smile. 'It was only a couple of thousand quid. Not much for a young man's life.'

Dani noticed one of the team waving in their direction. 'Here we go,' she announced, setting off towards the group of officers huddled together on the ground. 'Looks like we've finally got something.'

*

Bevan had taken a backseat whilst Carmichael informed Mrs Bannerman of the fate of her son. But Dani watched as the woman was led by a WPC along the corridor, presumably in the direction of the family liaison suite. She could have sworn she noticed the hint of a smile flicker across her wrinkled face. The sight made her involuntarily shiver.

'What's up?' Andy asked, moving across the office floor to stand beside his boss.

She nodded towards Mark's mum. 'That woman gives me the creeps. I swear she's enjoying this.'

'It's the notoriety Ma'am. The PM results are in.'

'Oh aye?'

'The body was pretty badly decayed, but the teeth are intact. The identification was straightforward. The pathologist noted a shattered jaw and cheekbone, along with several broken ribs. She's willing to confirm that Bannerman was beaten to death.'

'I wonder if Eric always intended to kill the guy, or it was an accident, like he told Craig?'

'Either way, Fisher was a murderer. He just didn't happen to murder his wife and kids.'

Dani turned to face her DC. 'So we're not looking for Mark Bannerman as our serial killer. Then who the hell is he, Andy, and how do we find him?'

Webber looked up from his computer screen. 'There's a military base just north of Dunblane. It's on the edge of the Trossachs National Park.'

'What are we waiting for?' Dani demanded. 'Let's go and check it out.'

*

The clouds had lifted, leaving a glorious late afternoon. The Larich Army Base was set right back from the road between Dunblane and Crieff. If it wasn't for the tall fencing which enclosed this area of scrubland, you'd barely know that it was there.

The base commander was expecting them. Calder stopped the car at a checkpoint and a man in uniform examined his ID, before directing them towards a series of pre-fabs scattered in the shadow of a hillside.

Colonel Ross Parker emerged from one of the tatty buildings to greet them. 'Welcome to Larich,' he announced. 'Please come inside.'

Bevan and Calder followed him obediently.

'So, what can I do to assist the City and Borders police?' Parker sat behind his desk, leaning forward expectantly.

Dani took a breath, knowing that what they had was thin. 'We are investigating a series of murders that have taken place across eastern Scotland. We have reason to believe that these crimes have been committed by a single individual. Certain intelligence that we've gathered indicates this person may have a military connection. It's also likely that our perpetrator lives somewhere within this region.'

Parker lifted an eyebrow ironically. 'Are you trying to suggest, DCI Bevan, that I have a serial killer on my base?'

'Not necessarily.' Dani sighed. 'This person may not still be serving in the military. I really need to take a look through your records, sir. This man is incredibly dangerous and could kill again at any time.'

Parker appeared to be considering this. 'I can let you take a look through the personnel files. It should give you the men's service history too. But I'll tell you now that I'm very sceptical about your theory, which I suspect is all it is. We have psychologists here at the base whose job it is to assess the men on a regular basis. We would be able to pick up on any changes in behaviour. I'll get Corporal Laing to assist you with the material. He's my archivist.'

'Thank you Colonel. I really appreciate it.'

Chapter 44

The boys were at school and the house was quiet. Louise padded around thoughtfully, picking up discarded pyjama bottoms and clearing away the mess left by breakfast.

She'd arranged to meet Laura for a coffee in town. Louise wasn't that bothered about seeing her but she felt that it might keep her occupied for a few hours and prevent her from ringing Davy. The last time she met her lover, they'd agreed to cool things off for a while. Louise finally realised how much she had to lose by allowing the situation to carry on.

Davy had seemed really upset, angry even. Louise had to promise him that they could hook up again whilst Fergus was away on a stag weekend. She had no intention of sleeping with him, but they could talk.

After completing the housework, Louise pulled on her jacket and headed out of the door. She caught a bus into town. It stopped outside the place she was meeting her friend. Laura was already inside.

Louise painted on an enthusiastic smile and pushed through the door to join her.

'I can't believe how much weight you've lost,' Laura announced, by way of a greeting. 'Are you doing some kind of keep fit at home?'

'Something like that,' Louise commented dryly.

'Whatever it is, it's bloody well working.' The woman waved vigorously at the waitress. 'I'm having a cake, how about you?'

'Yeah, go on.' Louise's vision was drawn towards the bay window of the café. For a moment, she was sure she'd seen a man standing outside watching them. Now he'd gone.

'Did you see the photo of us in the local paper? Dan thought we looked terrific, like real yummy mummies. I think he was quite proud. What did Fergus think?'

'Yes, he said we looked nice.' Louise absent-mindedly took a bite from the slice of Victoria Sponge that had been placed in front of her.

Her companion shot her hand out and caught hold of Louise's arm. 'Hey, Lou, what's going on here? You've been so distant the last few weeks. Are you sure things are okay at home?'

Louise caught the eye of her friend, who she immediately sensed already knew everything. 'I've been seeing someone.'

'I bloody knew it.'

'It's over now. I've been totally insane. I was just so lonely, dealing with the boys all by myself. They were playing up badly back then and never went to bed when I asked them to. When this guy came along and was kind to me I was like putty in his hands.'

Laura sat back and cradled her mug. 'You don't need to justify yourself to me. I did the same thing when Alice was a toddler.'

'*Really*? I never had the slightest clue.'

'He was a stay at home dad who I met at a soft play centre.' She began to laugh heartily. 'How sad is that?'

'What was he like?'

'He was lovely, still is I expect. We both needed the company – or comfort, more like. But after a while, you come to your senses.'

'Did you ever tell Dan?'

'Come on, how would that have helped? If I was running off with this other guy, I would have told him, otherwise, you keep it to yourself. Nobody has to get hurt.'

Louise slowly sipped her cappuccino, wondering if she would be able to extricate herself quite so easily.

*

The sun was setting outside the Larich Barracks. There were a hundred and forty soldiers on the base and they'd been through the files of half of them. Dani had to disagree with Colonel Parker, she actually felt that at least a dozen of the men she was reading about were candidates for developing into a serial killer.

There were plenty of incidences of broken relationships and post-traumatic stress amongst the personnel at the camp. But for many of these men, the dates of the murders simply didn't fit. The soldiers were either fighting in the field or on duty here at the camp when the killings took place. The military life seemed far too regimented for one of these men to be able move around so freely.

'I think our best bet is ex-army,' Dani suggested. 'Let's concentrate on those men who've been pensioned off in the last ten years.'

'Good idea,' Calder agreed. 'One of them may have decided to settle down nearby.'

Dani went outside to stretch her legs. The air was crisp and cold. It was just possible to see the outline of the Trossachs mountain range in the distance, against the grey sky.

The phone in the DCI's pocket began to ring, she glanced at the screen. 'Hi Phil.'

'Evening, Ma'am. I've been trying to call you for the last few hours.'

'There's probably no reception inside these lead-lined bunkers we're working in.'

Phil chuckled. 'I'm still working through the local

papers for the eastern region. I've identified about fifteen folk featured who have names associated with the Macdonald clan.'

'Great job. Can you e-mail them all through to me? I'll pick up the details when I'm back at Fettes.'

'There was something else, too. I thought it might be worth your while to get back in touch with DI Alexander, to assist you with your current lead.'

'Why is that?'

'Because Gordon was in the army before he joined the police. He'd signed up at sixteen, but when his dad died a few years later, he switched to the force. I think it was always his father's idea that he become a soldier. It wasn't really Gordon's calling.'

'Okay, that's useful information, Phil. The DI may well be able to help us.'

Chapter 45

Fergus Keene had taken the Friday off work and headed to the airport just after breakfast. The stag party were off to Stockholm for the weekend. Louise couldn't quite understand why the men would want to visit a place that would be even colder than Scotland. Fergus informed her they would be inside bars and restaurants the whole time so it didn't make much difference what the climate was like. Louise wanted to tell her husband not to go into any strip joints, but the hypocrisy would have been too much. She simply kissed him tenderly and told him to take care.

The boys had been really good since she'd picked them up from school. They'd found themselves some tasks to do and got on with them quietly. There'd been no squabbling, even at teatime.

Louise padded up the stairs and started running a bath. When she wandered into Jamie's room to get his clean pyjamas from a drawer her mobile phone started to ring.

'Hi Davy,' she replied, without enthusiasm.

'Lou, can I come over later? I really want to talk to you.'

'I'm not sure what it's going to achieve.'

'Please. I've got a proposition for you. I just need you to hear me out.'

She sighed. 'I'll have to get the kids to bed first. Wait until nine, when they're sure to be asleep. Come round the back and tap on the kitchen window, okay?'

'I will. And Louise, I love you.'

*

Dani had left Andy Calder at the Barracks, going through the personnel files with Corporal Laing. The DCI had decided to drive up to Dundee. Phil's tip seemed like a good one. No one in Bevan's team really had much of an idea of how to get into the mind of a soldier. If they were going to second-guess this monster, they needed all the insights they could get. The Corporal assured Dani they'd find Andy a bed for the night.

It was getting late by the time she reached the police headquarters. The lights on the bridge were being reflected back in the still waters of the River Tay. Bevan was hopeful that Gordon might still be at work. The guy had nothing to go home for.

Dani showed her warrant card to the middle aged woman on the reception desk, who remembered her. 'I'm not sure where DI Alexander has been this afternoon, Ma'am. But he's not clocked out just yet. Why don't you go up to the department and wait. You know where it is?'

The DCI nodded gratefully as the lady buzzed her though the security gate. Bevan took the lift to the serious crime floor. The lights had already been dimmed, the illuminations from the sprawling city itself being the only thing guiding Dani's way to Gordon's desk in the far corner.

As she sat down in the man's comfortable leather chair, Dani noted that only a couple of officers were still there, bent low over their desks, desperately trying to complete their paperwork and begin their Friday night.

Bevan swivelled gently back and forth, admiring

the neatness of the work surface before her. Then Dani's gaze rested on a set of photographs. One was of a woman in her early thirties, her hair dark and sleek, an attractive smile on her face. The others were of two children. Dani caught her breath at how very young they looked. There were two girls, one in a summer dress, playing in a garden full of flowers, the other just a wee toddler, sat squarely on a picnic blanket, with a set of bricks lying discarded between her podgy thighs.

Dani felt the tears welling up in her eyes once more, at the sight of these adorable youngsters. Then her vision was drawn to what lay beyond this pretty garden, to the dark outline of a distant mountain range, its peaks and troughs strangely familiar. Bevan snatched the frame off the desk and examined the scene more closely, reaching into her pocket for a mobile phone and rapidly starting to dial.

Chapter 46

Louise pulled the plug out, listening to the fierce gurgling of the murky water, as it span its way down the drain. She returned to Ben's room to find that her wee boy had switched off the light of his own accord and was wriggling down under the covers.

His mother moved silently across the room and bent over to kiss the top of his head.

'Night, Mum,' he murmured.

Louise could have wept. Maybe her little boys were finally growing up. Jamie was already asleep. She knew he would be. He was out like a light as soon as his head hit the pillow - that was the expression her mother always used about her youngest grandson.

Confident that the boys were settled, Louise made her way back downstairs. She glanced at the clock above the fireplace. It was half past eight. She didn't have very long.

The leftovers of a lasagne were covered with plastic wrap in the fridge. Louise went into the kitchen and dished some out, popping the plate in the microwave for five minutes. Before it pinged, she poured herself a glass of wine, hoping to be a bit tipsy by the time Davy showed up.

Fergus had called at the kids' teatime to say they'd arrived safely. They were heading to a pub and then on to a nightclub. He claimed he wasn't looking forward to it. Louise put the hot plate down on the table and sat in front of it, picking at the congealed tomato and meat sauce. She heard the rattling of the bins down by the side of the house. 'For Christ's sake,' she muttered bitterly. 'He's bloody early.'

Louise finished off her wine in one gulp, fortifying herself for the awkward encounter to come. Standing up to go and open the back door, she heard a noise from upstairs. It was one of the boys calling for her. 'Shit, this is all I need.'

She jogged up the stairs two at time. Jamie was standing in his doorway, his face all flushed. 'I don't feel well, Mum,' he said, his voice sounding small and weak.

Louise scooped him up in her arms, feeling his forehead. 'You've got a bit of a temperature sweetheart. I'll give you a spoonful of the purple stuff then you can go back to sleep.' They went into the bathroom and Louise lifted the medicine bottle down from a shelf. Jamie swallowed it with a grimace. A crash came from downstairs.

'What was that?' The boy asked, looking alarmed. 'Is Dad back?'

'No, it's nothing sweetie. Off to bed.' Louise shuffled her son into his room and tucked him back in. 'Now, I want you to go straight to sleep, okay? If you want anything, give me a call, but under no circumstances are you to come down the stairs, understand?'

He nodded.

'Good. Sweet dreams, darling.' His mum pulled the bedroom door to, so that it was very nearly closed. As she passed Ben's room, she shut his completely.

Louise crept slowly back down, thinking that the ground floor seemed much darker than when she'd left it ten minutes ago. When she reached the living room Louise could see why, the kitchen light was off. Maybe the bulb had gone. Her eyes scanned the back garden for a sign of Davy. Hopefully, he would be sitting obediently in a garden chair, waiting for her to be ready to let him in.

For some reason, her gaze was drawn through the kitchen window to the new extension beyond. Louise's hand flew up to her mouth. It must have been a kind of optical illusion but it looked from her position as if somebody was standing in the centre of the room. This person was huge and dressed all in black.

Suddenly, this hideous figure started to move. It was progressing at speed towards the sitting room. Louise's first instinct was to head for the stairs. She had to cut him off and protect her boys. She belted for the bottom step, seeing that terrifying dark shadow, shifting at a horrifying pace, from out of the corner of her eye.

Before Louise could get any further, she was brought to the ground, her chin hitting the skirting board with a painful thump. She wriggled as much as she could, but the weight on top of her was just too great.

Louise felt the cold, sharp edge of a blade, pressing against the soft skin of her neck. She closed her eyes tight shut, praying that the only target for this monster was her. She pleaded with some sort of faceless deity that this man would spare her babies.

Bracing herself for the worst, Louise felt the knife suddenly loosen in her attacker's grasp. If anything, the weight bearing down upon her became even greater.

'Louise! Louise! Are you okay?'

She managed to twist herself around and help Davy to shift this horrible thing off her. When she was able to free herself, Louise leapt up into the young man's arms.

'Oh my God, oh my God! I thought he was going to kill me!'

'He can't hurt you now my darling, I promise.'

'What did you do?'

'He was about to slit your throat Louise, I didn't have any choice.'

'What did you do to him, Davy?'

'I took a knife from the kitchen drawer and I put it in his back.'

Chapter 47

'Is he dead?' Dani stood over the body, her mouth set in a grim line.

The paramedic shook his head. 'There's a weak pulse.'

'Then let's get him in the ambulance. I want this bastard alive.'

DCI Bevan glanced around her. Louise Keene was sitting in the back of a squad car. The woman's two sons were wrapped in blankets and nestled in her arms. She hoped someone had called Joy and Bill. They'd want to be here as soon as possible.

A youngish man with shaggy brown hair was sitting on the front step of the house, with a plain clothed policeman asking him questions. Dani walked over to join them.

'This is David Burns. He was the one who knifed the attacker.'

'Thank you detective, I'll handle this.'

The policeman nodded and left them to it.

Dani squatted down on the step next to him. She noticed the man was shivering.

'I had to do it,' he said through chattering teeth. 'The guy was on top of her. He was about to cut her throat.'

Bevan laid a hand on his arm. 'I know you did. The person who attacked Mrs Keene is very dangerous. Once he'd killed Louise, he would have moved on to her children. But I need to ask you what you were doing there. How were you able to come to her aid so quickly?'

Davy glanced towards the woman sitting in the police car. 'Louise and I have been having an affair. We met when I was building their extension. Mr Keene doesn't know anything about it. He's away this weekend, so I insisted that I come over after the boys were in bed. I knew that Lou didn't really want me to. I was running a bit late. When I reached the back window I saw this monster on top of Louise. I kicked the back door in and grabbed a knife from the cutlery drawer. I swear I hardly thought about what I was doing.'

'You struck him once, Davy. That's self-defence. I've got a sense he's going to pull through anyway.'

The young man turned to look at her, his handsome face illuminated by the streetlights. 'For some reason, that doesn't actually make me feel better.'

*

There were two policemen on guard outside the door of the hospital room. Dani was sitting on one of the plastic chairs opposite as Andy Calder carried two cups of coffee along the silent corridor.

'Thanks,' she said quietly.

Andy dropped down into the seat beside her. 'Any news?'

'He's out of danger. The knife did penetrate his heart but the surgeon who operated on it thinks they've managed to stabilize the wound.'

'It's funny how none of his victims had the same luck.'

'I don't think that funny is the word I'd use.'

'How did you work out it was him?'

'When I went to the Dundee headquarters, I was sitting at Gordon's desk. He had photos of his wife and kids out on display. One was obviously taken in the garden of their home. In the background were hills of the Trossachs National Park. I still didn't know then that it was him, but it prompted me to give DC Webber a call. I asked him to find out everything there was to know about Detective Inspector Gordon Alexander.'

'What did Webber discover?'

'After the crash that killed his wife and daughters, Gordon spent several months in a psychiatric unit near Stirling. He simply had a total breakdown. But a year later, he was back on the force. According to Webber, Gordon's father was an officer in the Black Watch. He'd served his country in the Korean War. Phil said that Gordon's father had wanted his son to follow in his footsteps, but he'd chosen the police force instead. And look what happened as a result of going against his father's wishes? His whole family got wiped out.'

'But that had nothing to do with Gordon deciding on the police over the army. It's just one of those things – a random tragedy.' Andy sipped his milky drink.

'Yes, to us. But Gordon Alexander was completely devastated by his wife's accident. I think it distorted his entire world view. He decided to make amends to the memory of his dad by destroying all those who were responsible for undoing his father's work. He wanted to obliterate the descendants of the clans who were disloyal to the Union - and the army who were given the job of protecting it.

For a long time, this desire would have just been fantasy. Then, one day, he spotted a newspaper article. He saw three generations of traitors – Wheelans and Fishers. For reasons known only to him, this was when he decided to turn fantasy into reality.

It turns out that the Alexander family home

wasn't far from Dunblane. It's a remote country house that Webber says DI Alexander never sold. The man has a rented flat in the centre of Dundee, but I reckon Gordon must have been using the house as his real base. City and Borders are sending a couple of squad cars up there with a warrant to take a look around. I'd be interested to hear what they find there. Perhaps that's where Gordon kept the gear he used for the murders, or maybe the house is simply some kind of mausoleum to his wife and daughters. I can imagine the latter being the case. I believe that first and foremost, Gordon Alexander had been a devoted family man. When his family were so cruelly taken from him, Alexander was utterly broken. His destructive fantasy about preserving the Union crept in to take the place of the terrible grief and guilt he felt - not that I'm trying to excuse the things he did.'

'It makes the murder of the two wee Fisher twins more difficult to comprehend – why did he have to kill them?'

'He was setting out to destroy all the descendants of the clan, including future generations. But I don't think Gordon could quite bring himself to use the knife on the twins. They were the same age as his youngest daughter had been when she died. All Gordon could do was to hold their heads under the water until they stopped breathing. He took all his rage out on Peggy, Callum and Eric.'

'We know from Fisher's letter to his lawyer that Gordon forced him to plunge a knife into his wife and son. This helped to distort the forensic evidence. But Eric's account never seemed to fit with the times of death recorded by the pathologist. How did Gordon manufacture that?'

'Gordon Alexander is a senior policeman. He knows how a crime scene is worked. He could easily have restrained Peggy Fisher and come back for her later, after he'd killed Callum. All he had to do was confuse Eric, so that his version would be contradictory and he would get the blame for the murders.'

'So in the case of the Fishers, Gordon was hoping to place the blame on somebody else.'

'Yes, he wanted to avoid detection so that he could keep on with his grisly task. In each case, he's skilfully thrown us off the trail, because he's so forensically aware. But he must have been concerned after Eric Fisher was released. The man would have stopped at nothing to track down the butcher of his family.'

One of the policemen turned to glance through the window of the hospital room. 'He's shifting about, Ma'am. I think he might be waking up.'

'Andy, go and call a nurse. I'm going in.'

Gordon Alexander had been placed on his front, his head turned to one side. A thick bandage was taped across his broad back. Those big, strong hands were positioned by his sides.

Dani walked along the bed, stopping when she could see his face. The man's eyes were open.

'You've been in surgery. The doctors think you'll make a full recovery.'

Gordon grunted an acknowledgement.

Dani stared hard at his expressionless face, which she'd once thought so kind and compassionate. The detective pulled across a chair and sat down, leaning in closer. 'Tell me Gordon. What had Louise Keene, Callum Fisher or Morna Murphy ever done to you? Or all the others for that matter?'

The man did not respond.

'Those poor little children. The girls in the bath. That must have been really tough. I bet you had second thoughts then?'

Dani noticed his eyes flicker back and forth. She'd hit a nerve. 'Did Kyla and Skye remind you of your own little girls – as they looked up at you with their innocent, wide eyes?'

Gordon Alexander suddenly reared up, nearly dislodging the drip attached to his arm. Dani stumbled backwards, just out of his reach.

At this moment, the police guards charged in, followed by the doctor, who shot the detective a suspicious glance. 'I hope you've not been upsetting my patient? He's a very ill man.'

Dani placed her hands in the air and strode confidently towards the door. 'Don't worry, I've said my piece. I shan't be bothering him again.'

Chapter 48

'This is a bloody embarrassment for the police force.' DCS Angus Nicholson paced up and down the carpet in front of Dani Bevan's desk.

'It would be worse if DI Alexander were still out there, slaughtering people undetected.'

'Yes, of course.' Nicholson glanced in her direction. 'Well done for your part in this. It will be duly noted upstairs. You've managed to steer us clear of quite a few cock-ups in the process of this investigation. Thank you, Danielle.'

Dani dipped her head in acknowledgement.

'You realise that if you were to pursue a promotion at this point in time, your performance in this case would mean it was looked upon favourably.'

'What sort of promotion?'

'I hear that Urquhart might be retiring, in which case, they will be looking for a new superintendent at City and Borders.'

'*Edinburgh*?' Dani immediately thought about James.

Nicholson let out one of his rare chuckles. 'You make it sound like I'm proposing a move to Vladivostok. It isn't actually that bad. My wife hails from the east coast, you know.'

'It isn't that. It's just the idea of the change. I'd miss the team and working in the field.'

The DCS nodded. 'It's something to think about. Discuss it with your father, he'll provide you with good counsel I'm sure.'

Nicholson swept from the room, leaving Dani to her own meditations. She barely even noticed Phil and Andy slipping into the office after their superior had gone. Phil Boag collapsed onto the sofa whilst Andy remained standing.

'I keep running through all the times I spent with Gordon at the training academy. I simply cannot see how the man I knew back then could have turned into a serial killer.'

'It wasn't the same man, not really. The death of his wife and children sent him quite mad. He now lives in a delusional world of his own making,' Dani replied evenly. 'Much as I want to see Alexander punished properly for all the terrible things he's done, I also believe it should be recognised that the man is very probably mentally ill. The officers from City and Borders who went to the Alexander house on the edge of the Trossachs National Park said the place was horribly creepy. The girls' bedrooms had been left as if they were about to return at any moment. There were even wrapped gifts deposited about the place for them, with little handwritten labels attached.'

Phil visibly shuddered. 'It doesn't bear thinking about.'

'If he gets himself an expensive enough lawyer, you can bet your life they'll claim mental incapacity at the trial,' Andy declared.

Dani looked suddenly awkward. Her DC shot his boss a suspicious glance.

'Don't tell me that Sally Irving-Bryant is going to represent the bastard?' Andy was aghast.

'I believe they've already met a couple of times, since Gordon's been on remand. It is Sally's job.'

'You'd have thought Ms Irving Bryant would have learnt her lesson after her brush with Eric Fisher. Now, Gordon Alexander really *is* evil.'

'Do you truly believe that, Andy?' Phil asked his colleague, genuinely interested to know. 'Hasn't Gordon simply been sent mad by the misfortunes that life has thrown at him?'

Andy shook his head solemnly. 'No Phil, we've all had misfortunes thrown at us in life, some of us become depressed or hit the bottle, some sods might even hit their wives, but no one does what he did. The guy's evil, no question about it.'

Phil fell silent, obviously not willing to enter into an argument over the point.

Dani had been a policewoman for a long while and had seen many awful things in her career, but in this case she couldn't find the compassion that she might normally had done, for victim and perpetrator alike. In her heart of hearts, Dani knew that Calder was absolutely right.

Chapter 49

Fergus Keene unwrapped the bunch of flowers he'd brought home and carefully trimmed the stems, placing them into a vase of water before his wife came downstairs.

'They're lovely,' she said quietly. 'Thanks.'

Fergus moved across the room towards her, holding Louise's hands in his. 'What if I promise to work fewer hours? I'll be home more often, I promise. I'll make sure I'm back to help with bedtime. I know how difficult the boys can be at that time of day.'

'I just can't stay in this house,' she said flatly. 'And actually, Ben and Jamie are fine at going to bed now. That particular phase is over. I want to take them to Mum and Dad's for a bit. They'll be overjoyed to have us.'

'Okay, I can perfectly understand that. But don't cut me off Lou. Please don't tell me you're leaving to be with *him*.'

'I'll always be grateful to Davy, but I'm not going to continue my relationship with him.' Louise reached up to touch Fergus' cheek. 'I've been given a second chance. I want to spend some time considering what that means.'

The man felt tears spring to his eyes. 'I didn't protect you. I took you for granted.'

'Just let me take the boys to Mum's. You can come and see us whenever you like. Then, let's see what happens.'

'Can I hold you?'

'Of course.' Louise stepped forward into her

husband's embrace, feeling his body shudder with sobs. While Fergus wept, she looked over his shoulder at the extension they'd had built. It was shrouded in darkness. But Louise felt as if she could see the outline of that monstrous figure standing absolutely still, barely contained within its walls. It was a shadow that would always hang over this house. As far as Louise Hutchison was concerned, the sooner she and the boys were out of it, the better.

Chapter 50

The party was in full swing back at the main house. Dani and James had brought their drinks out into the garden and were sitting on the bench inside the summer house. The detective was leaning her weight against her companion.

'Have you thought any more about Nicholson's suggestion?' James stared into his glass of champagne, avoiding Dani's gaze.

'I've thought about little else.'

'You realise that if you were to move over this way, I'd have an excuse to buy that big rambling pile by the sea. There might actually be someone who could come and stay in it with me.'

Dani smiled, overwhelmed by an unexpected longing to live such an idyllic life with James. But following that was a wave of fear - the same terror which surged through her being like an electric shock whenever she considered the prospect of settling down and possibly having to provide her husband with children. 'Do you recall what happened to my mum?'

'Of course I do.' James slipped his free arm around her shoulders and gave her a squeeze.

'I've always been frightened of the same thing happening to me. It's why I've never sought out a long term relationship.'

'I don't want children from you, Dani. I just want you.'

She felt the tears prickling her eyes. 'But look at Grant and Sally in there, both of them celebrating the triumphs of their brilliant careers, but with no family. *Surely*, your parents must want grandchildren. I couldn't possibly take that chance away from them.'

James put his hand up to Dani's cheek and turned her face towards his. 'Don't I get a say in this? I'm not some prize stallion at a stud farm. I've never been all that certain I ever wanted kids. Come on, I'm nearly forty and I haven't settled down yet either. You aren't the only one here with baggage.'

Dani chuckled. 'I suppose that's true.'

'Look, I'm not entering into this relationship expecting you to provide me with offspring. But I could actually envisage *you* being the one who decides they want children in a few years from now. I happen to think you'd be a great mum. You do know there's no reason why you should have the same illness as your mother did. The treatment of depression has come on an incredible amount since then anyway. I really don't believe you should have to live in fear. It seems crazy in this day and age.'

Dani leant her head against his shoulder and took a sip of bubbly. 'Somebody else said that to me recently too.'

'Who was that?'

'Oh, it doesn't matter.' She shifted up. 'All that matters is that you both made a lot of sense.'

James bent down to place a soft kiss on her lips. 'Well, I hope that I made *more* sense.'

'Don't worry about that,' Dani giggled, pulling him closer, so he could kiss her again. 'There's really no contest on that score.'

*

238

If you enjoyed this novel, please take a few moments to write a brief review. Reviews really help to introduce new readers to my books and this allows me to keep on writing.
Many thanks,

Katherine.

If you would like to find out more about my books and read my reviews and articles then please visit my blog, TheRetroReview at:

www.KatherinePathak.wordpress.com

To find out about new releases and special offers follow me on Twitter:

@KatherinePathak

Most of all, thanks for reading!

≈

The Garansay Press